D0801898

ON THE FRINGE

ON THE FRINGE

Aaron and Charlotte Elkins

This first world edition published in Great Britain 2005 by
SEVERN HOUSE PUBLISHERS LTD of
9–15 High Street, Sutton, Surrey SM1 1DF.
This first world edition published in the USA 2006 by
SEVERN HOUSE PUBLISHERS INC of
595 Madison Avenue, New York, N.Y. 10022.

British Library Cataloguing in Publication Data

Elkins, Aaron J.
   On the fringe. - (Lee Ofsted mysteries)
   1.   Ofsted, Lee (Fictitious character) - Fiction
   2.   Women golfers - United States - Fiction
   3.   Detective and mystery stories
   I.   Title II. Elkins, Charlotte
   813.5'4 [F]

   ISBN-10 : 0-7278-6286-3

Typeset by Palimpsest Book Production Ltd.,
Polmont, Stirlingshire, Scotland.
Printed and bound in Great Britain by
MPG Books Ltd., Bodmin, Cornwall.

One

Wally Crawford swallowed the last of his after-dinner French vanilla-bean coffee, pushed his chair back from the table, stretched elaborately, yawned, and looked startled, or hoped that he did.

'Oh, no. Is today Thursday?'

'Yes, all day long.' His wife, Cookie, was finishing her own coffee as she rose from the dinner table.

'Nuts. Tomorrow's Friday?'

She looked at him. 'I wouldn't be surprised.'

'Damn.' Fearing that this lacked suitable emphasis, Wally repeated it – '*Damn!*' – and banged the table with his palm for good measure. 'I just realized. I have to go back to the office, can you believe it?'

Cookie paused in clearing the table and stared at him, incredulous. 'Now? *CSI Miami* comes on in fifteen minutes.'

'*CSI Miami* comes on every night. I can miss it for once.'

'No, those are different *CSI*s. But what's so important? What can't wait until tomorrow?'

Wally shook his head mournfully. 'The board's meeting first thing in the morning and I'm supposed to give them a progress report on the front-nine irrigation project.' This was true and Wally delivered it with appropriate conviction. 'I don't know why, but I kept thinking it was Wednesday all day today, and I never got anything ready for them.' This was a total fabrication, which made him glow with even greater sincerity.

Cookie, with the cups and saucers stacked in her hands, peered down at him, her eyes narrowed. 'Is that true?'

'Of course it's true. You think I want to go back?'

'You're not after those stupid treasure hunters again, are you?'

Wally rolled his eyes. 'Jeez, Cook . . .'

'Because remember what happened the last time.'

Wally nodded. It wasn't something he was likely to forget. Stubbing your toe on an out-of-alignment sprinkler head in the dark, falling flat on your face and breaking your nose was the kind of thing that stayed with you, especially when you'd been wearing a nose splint until two days ago, and your two black eyes were only now turning a marginally less livid shade of purplish-brown.

'Cookie,' he said humbly, 'you're completely in the right. Trust me, I may be dumb, but I am not crazy.'

'I don't know. I'm coming to the conclusion that it's the other way around.'

'Cookie, I am not planning to scare off any trespassers. I—'

'Good, because that's not your job. You're a golf pro, not a policeman. Why don't they go to the police with this?'

'You know the answer to that, Cook. A, they don't want the publicity, and B, what would the police do, patrol the place every night? All eighteen holes? To stop a little digging?'

'Well then, why don't they hire a security man to do it, if they're so worried about its getting torn up?'

He shrugged. She knew the answer to that too, just as well as he did: because the governing board of the Royal Mauna Kea Golf and Country Club, despite their individual and collective wealth, was constitutionally and instinctively penurious ('frugal' was their word for it), guarding the club's nickels and dimes like an eagle guarding its nestlings.

'Look, Cookie,' he said, all reasonableness, 'I am going down to the garage, I am going to get in the car, I am going to drive to the club, I am going to go to my office—'

'I don't know how you can stand going to that creepy old place at night. It's gloomy enough in the daytime.'

2

'The clubhouse is not gloomy, it's . . . stately. It's based on some old Scottish castle. Macbeth's castle or something.'

'That's what it looks like.' She raised her fingers like talons. '"Fire burn, and cauldron bubble." Woooo.'

He sighed. 'And when I get to my office, I am going to put together a progress report on the piping for holes seven, eight and nine. Then I am going to prepare a few PowerPoint slides for the meeting. And then I am coming straight home,'

She peered down at him, not wholly convinced. 'Is that a promise?'

'Yes.'

'Say it.'

'I just said it.'

'No, say "I promise."'

Another roll of the eyes, another shake of the head, and Wally's right hand came up as if he were swearing himself in. 'I absotively, posilutely promise,' he said, and stood up. Then he gave a final chuckle and an affectionate peck on her cheek while he checked in his pocket for the car keys. 'Jeez, Cookie, you'd think that after twenty years you'd trust me a little.'

'That's the problem,' she said. 'I know you.'

The first thing Wally did when he got to the condo's open-air parking garage was to raise the trunk lid of the Saab to make sure that this time he was prepared. First, the flashlight. He had put in two new nine-volt batteries that afternoon, but he flicked it on anyway, just to make sure. He wasn't going to fall over some stupid sprinkler head this time. The flashlight worked fine.

Then the shotgun, an old double-barreled job with exposed hammers. He looked over each shoulder to make sure nobody was there, then lifted it out and cracked it open. There, safely chambered, were two 12-gauge blank shells that would be louder than the real thing, if the clerk who'd sold them to him at the Kona Wal-Mart was to be believed.

He dropped two more shells into each of his two hip pockets

and grimly nodded his satisfaction. This time he was going to scare the living hell out of the bastards. He was going to give them a jolt that would ensure they'd never be back. And the word would get around soon enough, and keep the others away too. With his mouth set and his jaw muscles working, he started up the Saab, backed it out of its stall, turned it around, then drove slowly down the curving driveway, turned north on Queen Kaahumanu Highway and into the mild Hawaiian night for the fifteen-mile drive to the Royal Mauna Kea.

So they thought they could just walk in and dig up his beautiful, satiny, perfect greens and get away with it, did they? Well, they had another think coming.

According to the schoolbooks, the westernization of Hawaii began with the arrival of a boatload of New England missionaries in 1820, but the old-guard members of the Royal Mauna Kea Golf and Country Club track history from another seminal date: 1905, when visionary Scottish expatriate and millionaire Augustus Cumberland set out to prove that a verdant golf course could flourish along the lava-encrusted lowland flanks of the mighty Mauna Kea volcano on the far-off island of Hawaii. Flourish it did, and also became one of the Big Island's most elite and exclusive social establishments, with membership being restricted to male descendants of the founding members until well into the 1960s, when growing competition and declining membership – mostly due to age – forced it into a more democratic mode. In 1965, the first female member was admitted; in 1996, the first Hawaiian.

The clubhouse, a turreted, crenellated pile of somber gray granite imported from he didn't know where (the stuff didn't exist in Hawaii), was not really based on Macbeth's castle at Glamis, but its forbidding exterior would certainly have been better suited to the wintry blasts of the Isle of Arran than the warm breezes of the island of Hawaii. The plush, elegant interior, however, more than made up for it in Wally's opinion. The building had been designed and built in 1905 and 1906 by the American architect Nathan Wyndham, who was so taken with his creation that he sold his business, moved to Hawaii, bought a nearby sugar plantation, and became a valued club member. When Augustus Cumberland died in 1908, it was Wyndham who personally commissioned a club memorial for him from the great Louis Comfort Tiffany: the Cumberland Memorial Cup.

This gorgeous object was a two-foot-tall, exquisitely wrought silver urn decorated with looping, delicate traceries of rubies. On its face, set in a white onyx oval completely rimmed with pear-shaped yellow diamonds, was an ancient, enigmatic lava-stone figurine that had been dug up during the original landscaping of the golf course. Almost from the beginning the precious cup had been as much a source of worry as it was of pride, so much so that it was put on display only on special occasions and protectively secreted away the rest of the time. For one thing, it soon became worth far more than had been paid for it, since it turned out to be the last major piece on which Tiffany himself, and not his studio, had done the work. For another, the lava-stone figurine turned out to have significance for some of the island's loonier folks. One cult-like group in particular declared it to be the legendary, sacred Mana Stone, a relic carved from the 'flesh' of the great volcano by Kamehameha the Great himself. Unless it was returned to its 'mother,' the volcano, they insisted, the whole island would soon perish in a cataclysmic explosion of fire, lava and rock from deep within the earth's core.

Happily, this failed to occur, but not long after the Japanese attack on Pearl Harbor, the governing board of the club despondently announced that the cup had disappeared from its secret hiding place. Rumors prevalent at the time, however, suggested that the board knew exactly what had happened to it: it had simply been taken away and buried somewhere – very probably on the grounds of the country club – in anticipation of a Japanese invasion of the island. For a decade or so after the war the rumor hung on, generating an irritating succession of treasure hunters who thought nothing of clandestinely digging holes in the fairways, bunkers and greens, all in pursuit of the lost cup. Groundskeepers and maintenance men had been kept busy repairing pits, tunnels and trenches. Even the sacred precincts of the great clubhouse had been violated in the widespread belief that Wyndham had designed it with secret passages and hidey-holes, and who knew what might be concealed there?

But as memories dimmed the depredations gradually died away – until the previous January, when the Bishop Museum in Honolulu opened a well-publicized exhibit on the Arts and Crafts movement at the turn of the twentieth century and its effects on Hawaiian decorative arts. The exhibit catalogue featured a full-page photo of the cup and several paragraphs detailing its history, which were enough to bring the treasure seekers out again. And as if that hadn't been enough, Mauna Kea, which had been perfectly quiet for the last four thousand years, gave out with a few rumbling belches, bringing forth a new fringe end-of-the-world group that had then begun hassling the club, demanding that the cup, or at least the figurine, be produced and returned to the volcano before fiery death rained down upon man and his creations, most definitely including the Royal Mauna Kea Golf and Country Club. No doubt, they were responsible for some of the digging as well.

And all this came right in the middle of planning for the club's big, week-long Centennial bash. It was enough to make a man tear his hair out.

Wally Crawford didn't have enough hair to make tearing it out worth doing, but he had suffered plenty. He didn't give much of a damn about the old cup, but as the golf pro, he was responsible for the grounds, and he took the responsibility seriously. He genuinely loved the gorgeous course, and when he made his rounds some mornings and discovered a three-foot pit in the middle of once-perfect fairway – or, God forbid, one of the greens – it was as if they had gouged it right out of his heart. People thought that you just replaced the dug-out dirt, laid on some fresh sod, and everything was hunky dory again, but those were people who had no conception of the beauty of a smooth, flawless, even golf green and what it took to keep it that way. In reality, it took a year, often more, for the wounded turf to recover, and in the meantime you had a big, ugly, off-color, off-texture spot to mar the perfection and bring complaints from members who were sure their otherwise faultless putts had gone astray because of a blade of grass that bent in the wrong direction. Often enough, the grass never properly recovered, and a scar was left, like a horrible disfiguration on the silken back of a beautiful woman.

Well, it was payback time now.

Instead of turning in at the club's palm-lined driveway he continued a quarter of a mile past it to the immense Lani Kai Hotel, left the car in its parking lot and walked, shotgun satisfyingly heavy in one hand, the shielded, down-pointing flashlight in the other, on to the meandering maintenance track that defined the property line between the hotel and the club. From there, by criss-crossing the fairways at the right spots and using the footbridges over the man-made lake, he could cover the entire 6,800-yard course in under thirty minutes.

He began midway down the eighth fairway, walking straight across it, and then across the seventh, had a brief tour of the third, and crossed the Japanese footbridge to the first. Just as he reached the top of the curving bridge, the late-rising moon peeked out from above a low bank of sea clouds and lit the scene. He stopped to take it in. The lake in its serpentine channels gleamed like pewter, the fairways were like the soft, smooth pelt of some great, powerful animal – like a panther or a brushed and groomed thoroughbred race horse. How beautiful!

His outrage and determination grew. Clutching the shotgun more firmly, more resolutely, he continued over the bridge, his ears alert to any sound other than the distant, hissing surf. In his heart he was sure he was going to catch them in the act. Five nights had gone by now with no violation of the course. They were due; they would be out there. When the pale, flat disc of the moon emerged more fully, he saw with pleasure that it was a perfect circle. Great: a full moon. That made it certain: if not the treasure hunters, then at least the nuts would be out looking for the Mana Stone.

He turned off the flashlight. No sense in getting noticed until he wanted to get noticed. And with the moonlight, there was no danger now of tripping over a sprinkler head. It was at the tenth that he saw, or rather heard them. A low murmur of conversation – two people, no three – coming from the tee area a hundred yards or so to his right. He crept closer along the edge of the fairway. Yes, three men – Haoles? Hawaiians? He couldn't tell – apparently digging three separate holes a few yards apart. *Three* holes, for Christ's sake! For a brief moment he came close to wishing he had live ammunition in the chambers. When he was about fifty yards away he knelt and, barely breathing, eased back both hammers of the shotgun as quietly as he could. He was raising it to his shoulder and gathering breath in his chest for the terrible bear-like roar he had ready to accompany the first blast, when disaster struck.

His nerves must have been more on edge than he realized, because when the earth itself suddenly seemed to shudder, a great wave of panic shot up in him. An earthquake? A tsunami? Was Mauna Kea really erupting? But he had only a second to consider these possibilities before a dozen leaping jets of water came spiraling from the turf around him, the individual droplets gleaming and twisting in the moonlight like smelt in the sea. The sprinklers! Good God, how could he have forgotten to turn off the damn automatic sprinkler system? He heard the diggers exclaim and curse as well.

Angry with himself, with water running into his eyes, he ducked blindly back toward the rough, where at least he could have the minimal protection of trees and shrubs. He had only taken two steps when his ankle was caught hard by something and he was sent tumbling through the air in a near-complete somersault.

'Please, not another sprinkler head!' was all he had time to think before he came down on an irregular strip of black lava that lay between the fairway and the rough. Amazingly he landed on both feet – or at least his left foot – but it was the side of his foot and he was dismayed to hear a sharp snap, as if a dry branch had broken, and then his ankle collapsed under him. When he hit the ground, his finger must have tightened convulsively on the shotgun's triggers. The two barrels went ear-splittingly off into the night.

A sprawling, ludicrous figure, deafened, helpless, soaked through, and in rapidly intensifying pain, there was only one thought at the forefront of his mind.

How the hell was he going to explain this to Cookie?

Two

'**M**r Crawford's room?' Lee Ofsted asked.
'Down the hall – twenty-four, last room on the left,' said the middle-aged Hawaiian nurse, leaning on the counter and fingering the lanyard of her dangling glasses. Audrey N. Nakoa, RN, Ward Supervisor, said the nameplate on her starched and formidable bosom. 'Help yourself.'

There was something about the way she said it that made Lee pause. 'Has he been giving you trouble?' she asked, smiling.

'No, he's just . . .' The nurse slipped on the glasses and peered at Lee. 'Are you family?'

'No, an old friend.'

The nurse scrutinized her even more closely. Lee knew what she was thinking. At a shade under twenty-five, Lee looked even younger. From Audrey's point of view, that wasn't old enough to be anybody's 'old' friend. Still, she seemed satisfied with what she saw.

'Well, between you and me . . .' She leaned confidentially toward Lee, her elbows on the counter. 'He may be a very nice man – I'm sure he has a heart of gold—'

'Well, I don't know that I'd go as far as that,' Lee murmured.

'—but as a patient, he is . . . he is just so . . . so . . .' She stopped, at a loss for words.

'He can be difficult, I know,' Lee said sympathetically.

'Difficult? The man is hell on wheels. Fortunately, he's being discharged tomorrow – "sprung" is his charming term for it – so I may yet survive.'

Lee laughed. 'I'm sure you will.' She held up the 12-ounce Starbucks container she'd brought into the hospital with her. 'Okay if I bring this for him?'

'Sure. And listen, if he starts in with you, you have my permission to tell him where to get off. It'd do him good.'

'Will do,' Lee said.

Yeah, right, she said to herself. Twenty years his junior and enormously and gratefully in his debt, she had as much chance of successfully telling Wally to do something as she did of teaching an elephant to tapdance.

Wally Crawford had been beyond any doubt the most important person in her life when she was in the Army. While she'd been stationed at a small Army supply depot in Germany, Wally, a sergeant in the Air Force, had served as the golf instructor at the nearby Hahn Air Force Base. The base, like the supply depot, sat atop a long, desolate ridge above the Mosel River that the Germans wryly called the Hunsrück, which meant 'dog's back,' and it drew rain, fog, and wind the way its namesake drew fleas.

Hahn, like many other Air Force bases, had taken advantage of the otherwise unusable corridors paralleling its runways to lay out an adequate, if noisy, nine-hole golf course to make life a bit more livable for its frequently bored personnel. This had been of no interest to Lee until a two-dollar raffle ticket won her a golf weekend at the Army's R and R facility in Garmisch. Willing to give it a try, but hardly knowing the difference between a wedge and a waffle-maker, she had timidly made her way to the course's clubhouse on one of her days off, hoping to sign up for an introductory lesson.

Bluff and friendly, Wally had been wonderful. Not only did he give her a lesson and trustingly lend her a better set of clubs than she would have been given in Garmisch, he immediately sensed her natural talent and encouraged her to pursue it. For the remaining year of her service, the course and practice range became a second home to Lee. Wally, impressed with her ability to take the miserable weather in her stride, worked her hard and energetically. It had helped, of course, that she'd grown up in the misty, bracing air of Portland, Oregon, which wasn't really all that different from the Hunsrück's. It seemed natural to her that she should learn to play golf in conditions that purpled her ears and made her eyes water, on fairways that could have passed for marshes, and on greens – riddled with worm castings – that were so slow you could do your nails while waiting for your ball to roll into the hole. And although nothing had prepared her for the brain-piercing shrieks of the F-16s landing on the adjacent runways, she treated them as the character-builders they were. Not for her to 'miss short putts because of the uproar of butterflies in the adjacent meadow,' as P.G. Wodehouse had so memorably put it.

What she hadn't shared with Wally and many of the other base golfers – almost all male – were the numerous Scotch toddies they were in the habit of knocking back to warm up after a round. (They claimed it was in the spirit of tradition: legend had it that the reason a round of golf consisted of precisely eighteen holes was that eighteen was the number of 'nips' of Scotch – one to a hole – that an eighteenth-century hip flask contained.) But, like men anywhere else, they enjoyed having a young, lively, pretty blonde around to flirt with, to tease, and to listen to their stories. This despite her being not only a teetotaler, but a pretty straight-laced one at that, and even worse, beginning to regularly outplay them after only a couple of months' experience with a golf club.

The door to room twenty-four was open. There were two beds in it, one vacant and the other containing her old mentor. He was sitting up against a mass of pillows in the S-curved bed with his arms crossed, sourly watching a Jerry Springer show – 'My grandmother dresses like a hooker and my grandfather dresses like a pimp!' – and he looked like absolute hell. His legs were hidden by a sheet that was propped up over some kind of rack, but it was his face, with its two bruised, blackened raccoon eyes and swollen, painful-looking nose, that shocked her. And, like anyone else in a short-sleeved, collarless hospital smock that tied at the back of the neck, he looked shrunken and vulnerable.

She knocked gingerly to let him know she was there. He turned to glare at whoever it was, only to break into a gratifyingly genuine smile at seeing her.

'Lee! I didn't expect to see you till tomorrow, after they spring me.'

'Well, I was here, and I'm too jet-lagged to go out and paint the town red, so I thought, why not drop by and see how they're treating you.'

'Like a goddamn two-year-old,' he said grouchily. 'Pull up a chair.'

She moved a couple of fishing magazines from the nearest chair and slid it over to the bed. 'Now. How are you?'

'Great, wonderful,' he grumped. 'I got about ten pounds of pins and screws and wires in my ankle. Couldn't be better.' He pointed at her hand. 'I'm sure hoping that Starbucks is for me. What they give you here is dishwater.'

'Oh. Sorry.' She jumped up with the cup. 'Of course it's for you. A double-shot latte.'

'Ah, wonderful. Put one of those bendy straws in it, will you? If I spill anything on my smock, Nurse Ratchet will punish me.'

'Audrey? She didn't seem so bad.'

'You're not her patient,' Wally muttered.

'Wally, I have to ask you: what in the world were you doing out on the golf course in the middle of the night?'

He looked up at the ceiling. 'Oh, Jesus. Look, no offense, but I really don't want to go into it, okay? Maybe later. Because . . .' He paused for his first swig of coffee, swished it around his mouth with a quizzical expression, and swallowed. His expression softened. His whole body seemed to relax. 'There's *Scotch* in here!' he whispered, delighted.

'One of those tiny little bottles of Glenlivet – is that a good brand? I thought you might appreciate it.'

Wally had another swallow and lay back against his pillows with a sigh of contentment, the cup lovingly cradled against his midsection. 'God bless you, child. Now, what was it you wanted to know?'

'What you were doing out on the golf course in the middle of the night.'

'Well, it's a long story,' he said, but with the spiked coffee safe in his hands, he was no longer averse to telling it. 'First you have to understand what the Royal Mauna Kea is like. This place is as old-fashioned and traditional as you can get and the membership is full of hoity-toity New Englanders and a few ex-Brits who still think Queen Victoria's in charge, or at least wish she was. But, really, that's fine with me, even if it gets me in some hassles with the board. But that's beside the point. Everything was going fine there until the Bishop Museum had their damn art show and the Mauna Kea volcano started making noises—'

Lee put up her hand. 'Wait, I'm already lost. The Bishop Museum in Honolulu? The volcano? What do they have to do with the golf club?'

Wally laughed. 'Maybe I'd better start at the beginning. You got a little time?'

Twenty minutes later, as Wally regretfully tipped the cup to get the last dregs, he came to the end of the story. 'And so there I was out there trying to catch some of those miserable scumbags in the act and scare the sh— scare the hell out of them, only I forgot to turn the sprinkler system off, and I wound up tripping over one of them and taking a hell of a fall. I landed on my feet, but I didn't land right. Obviously.'

Lee nodded at his swollen, discolored features. 'Looks as if you landed on your face too.'

'No, that's from a couple of weeks ago,' he said, then dropped his chin to his chest and mumbled something else.

'What?'

More mumbling, sheepish and sulky.

Lee stared incredulously at him. 'Did I just hear you say

14

you did the same thing two weeks ago? You tripped over a sprinkler head *twice?*'

He fidgeted. 'Well, you know, it's not as if it was the same sprinkler head.'

'But still . . .'

'Lee, honey, I can't thank you enough for coming out and offering to help with the club Centennial events – the indoor putting championship and that kind of thing.'

Well, if he didn't want to talk about it, that was fine with her. She could certainly understand. 'Offering?' she countered. 'My arm still hurts from being twisted. As I remember it, when you called and told me about your, um, accident – the first accident, I guess it was – I know I asked if there was anything I could do to help, but that wasn't what I had in mind. I'd be a disaster trying to run an indoor putting championship, whatever that might be. I know absolutely zilch about these fancy country club "events." I've never even belonged to one. I learned my golf on an Air Force base in the Hunsrück, remember? I don't believe we ever had an indoor putting championship.'

'You'll be fine, I have complete confidence in you. They tell me I'll be up and around at least a little in a day or two, so I'll be able to take care of a lot of the office stuff – arrangements, details, you know. They just don't want me out on the course, but if you really need me . . .'

'Oh, I'm just giving you a hard time. I don't want you rushing things on my account. I can handle things out on the course itself, and a friend of mine, Peg Fiske, flew in with me. She's on her local club board. She loves to do events. And she's a management consultant, so she knows how to run things. She'll do a great job handling the indoor putting, if that's all right with you.'

'All right with me? Are you kidding? That's great! And when does your boyfriend arrive for the wedding?'

'Fiancé,' Lee said, relishing the pleasure of the word and even blushing a little.

'Pardon me, fiancé. So when does this Graham character

15

arrive? Will I have to explain the birds and bees to him?'

'Um, well, no, I don't think—'

There was a quick double tap on the door. They both turned to see Audrey Nakoa standing there.

'Good afternoon, Nurse Ratchet,' Wally said.

'Don't be impolite,' said Audrey. 'I'm afraid visiting's over for now, Miss. You can come back after dinner.'

Wally shook his head. 'Jeez, they have the nerve to call it dinner.'

'I guess I'll get going,' Lee said. 'I told Peg I'd join her for a soak in the hot tub.' She leaned over and, on impulse, kissed him on the cheek. 'I'll check in later. Anything I can bring?'

Wally handed her the empty Starbucks cup. 'Another one of these would be great. Just like this one'

'No caffeine after dinner,' Audrey warned him.

'Oh, I didn't realize that, Nurse Ratchet,' Wally said docilely. 'All right then, exactly the same, only decaf.'

'That's better,' Nurse Nakoa said.

Three

'Aaaahhhhh,' Peg Fiske sighed as she settled slowly into the still, turquoise water of the volcanic-rock-lined hot tub, basked quietly for a moment in the warmth, then leaned over to hit a recessed button in the curving wall. The jets started up with a whoosh, and the water swirled with lovely, champagne-like skeins of bubbles.

'I'm in heaven,' she said.

'Sure looks like it to me,' said Lee. 'Let me join you.' She slipped her feet out of her sandals, unwrapped her swimsuit cover and dropped it on to the nearest deckchair, then walked gingerly down the rough stone steps into the water.

'Ouch. Hot.'

'It is?' said Peg. 'Gee, I wonder if that's why they call it a hot tub. Don't worry, you'll get used to it.'

'Mm, I'm already used to it,' Lee said with a sigh, sinking down on to the circular ledge along the rim, formed with a comfortable angled back rest to allow the bather to sit with neck and head out of the water. She could practically feel the heat and the bubbles knead away what was left of her travel fatigue. 'Heaven is right,' she said, closing her eyes and leaning her head and shoulders against the rim. 'What a place.' She slid down, crocodile-like, so that only her nose and eyes were above the water. Bubbles tickled her upper lip.

The Outrigger's hot tub looked as if it had been plunked in the middle of a lush jungle. Tropical vegetation was everywhere. Above them, on the hillside, water cascaded over stone ledges into a series of clear pools on its way to them.

Below, a continuing series of twinkling, meandering runnels and pools led down and away to the brilliant-white crescent of Anaehoomalu Beach, which Lee had yet to try to pronounce, let alone to visit. Any intimations of untamed jungle, however, were put to rest by the handsome hotel buildings behind them, and by the artful plantings everywhere on the grounds. Jungle, yes, but jungle that had been brought under control by human hands and arranged for human pleasure.

'It's not bad,' agreed Peg, who was a great deal more used to such surroundings than was Lee. 'So how did it go at the hospital?'

Lee raised her head enough to speak. 'Hm? Wha'?'

'Don't go to sleep on me now. How's your friend?'

Reluctantly, Lee made herself sit up a little straighter, so that her chin was out of the water. 'Wally? He's grumpy as hell, but he'll survive, and, knowing him, he'll be back in business in no time.'

'Does that mean you won't have to take over for him after all?'

'Don't I wish, but unfortunately, no. The man's got a shattered ankle, Peg. He thinks he'll be up and at 'em in no time, but he's not going to be able to get around easily for weeks. Anyway, he does want me to run some of the events – like this indoor putting championship they're having tomorrow.' She sighed. 'I'm happy to help him, but it's not the kind of thing I'm very good at – or comfortable with.' She looked across the small pool at her friend. 'I was hoping, well . . .'

'Sure, I'll run it for you if you want, as long as Wally approves.'

'I'm sure he will,' Lee said, seeing no good reason to mention that the proposition had already been put to Wally and that he had indeed approved. 'Peg, I really appreciate your coming early to help out.'

Peg's foghorn hoot of laughter startled a *nene* – a small Hawaiian goose – at the edge of one of the pools out of its doze. 'Yeah, this is a heck of a hardship. You owe me big time.' She sank contentedly even deeper into the water. 'Truthfully, though – no offense, of course – but why exactly does he want you to take over everything for him, rather than just asking some assistant pro from one of the other courses? The coast is littered with them. Surely somebody would help him out in a case like this.'

'Yes, I know, but it seems as if this is rather an old-fashioned club, full of ancient skinflints, and I think he's afraid to bring in some younger guy and have the board like him too much. Wally's contract comes up for renewal next month, and they could naturally get a less senior guy cheaper. And since I was coming out anyway to be the celebrity guest, he figured I could do it. And I do owe him.'

She smiled to herself. Celebrity guest. She'd said it so nonchalantly, and Peg hadn't batted an eyelash either. My, how times change.

She'd met Peg, an avid weekend golfer, when Peg been one of the paying amateurs in Lee's foursome at a pro-am tournament in her rookie year on the Women's Professional Golf League tour. Despite a vast distance in age, class, and income – Peg was forty-three, Lee would turn twenty-five this month; Peg's mother and father had been a psychiatrist and a professor while Lee's father laid concrete and her mother was a housewife and part-time food-server in a school cafeteria; Peg was married to a successful engineer and ran her own $800,000-a-year management-consulting business out of Albuquerque while Lee's best year until recently had netted her $9,500 after expenses – despite all this, the two of them had hit it off from the first and had, surprisingly, become fast friends. From the beginning Peg had loyally thought of her as a star (in the making, she might have allowed, if pushed.) And in fact Lee's three-year-old career had been on a solid, if slow, progression upward, with enough flashes of exhilarating – and even brilliant – play to keep her working hard and dreaming that she would some day truly be a star. And that day had arrived unexpectedly just two short months ago.

Lee had won the 'Rocky' slot on the American team – the one slot chosen by lottery as opposed to merit – for the Stewart Cup Tournament, one of golf's premier international events. Even more unbelievably, she had somehow managed to score the pressure-laden point that had brought the Americans roaring back from defeat at the last minute, thereby bringing the cup home from Great Britain for the first time in six years. Among the results had been a middle-high five-figure endorsement contract from Comet Golf that still took her breath away whenever she thought of it. More important, seeing her play in the tournament had helped Graham Sheldon, her fiancé, to finally comprehend the intensely stressful and competitive core of professional golf and to really, truly grasp how much the game meant to her, how deep a part of her life it was. This new understanding had given her the courage to do something she'd been waffling about for months: to do what Graham had been quietly urging for a while now, and mix career and marriage. Wally's original invitation to Hawaii had fortuitously arrived just then, giving the two of them a perfect opportunity for a lovely, quiet wedding in the Islands, which she'd never visited. Things weren't as quiet as she'd anticipated, but the wedding was still on, and in five short days Peg would be her matron of honor.

Peg's cheerful bugle of a voice broke into her thoughts. 'So if you screw up, so much the better. It'll make Wally look good.'

Lee laughed. 'I suppose that's one way of looking at it. Wally's a great guy, Peg. You'll like him.'

'I'm sure. Listen, did you find out what in the world he was doing wandering around out there with a shotgun in the dark?'

'I sure did, and you'll love it.' She filled Peg in on the goings-on, past and present, at the Royal Mauna Kea Golf and Country Club.

Peg whistled as Lee finished her story. 'This is really going to be an interesting few days.'

'Me first!'

'No, *me* first!'

The outraged cries came from a pair of girls, perhaps eight and ten years old, who were elbowing each other in an effort to be first into the hot tub. Behind them, their frazzled-looking parents, also headed for the tub, were attempting to mediate.

'Kimberly was first in the swimming pool,' their mother said, 'so Ashley goes first here. That's only fair.'

'Ha-ha,' said the smaller one, presumably Ashley.

'You always take her—' started the other girl.

'That's it!' said the father. 'Enough already. One more word and we turn around and go right back to Cleveland. I mean it!'

'But, Daddy, we just—'

'Oh, baloney,' muttered the older one, more experienced in the ways of her father. 'We are not going back. Not after all the money we paid.'

'Kimberly, I'm warning you . . .'

'Darn, you mean we don't get this all to ourselves?' Lee whispered to Peg.

'Afraid not. A shame, isn't it? What do you say we go get something to eat? I think I'm just about braised to perfection anyway.'

'Oh, I hope you're not leaving on our account?' the mother inquired prettily.

'No, no, of course not,' they assured her.

Once they'd wound themselves in their wraparounds and were walking back along a curving, frangipani-bordered path toward their rooms, Peg took a familiar, benignly dictatorial tone with Lee. 'Now you listen to me, my girl. You are not to concern yourself with the indoor putting affair or similar silly-season goings-on. You are to rely on me for such things. I have been captain of the women's golf club at Cottonwood Creek for four years now. You name it, I've organized it. So leave it to me. There is *nothing* I don't know about running amateur golfing events – the weirder the better.'

*   *   *

21

Or so she'd thought before coming face to face with the rules of the Royal Mauna Kea Golf and Country Club's Annual Indoor Putting Championship, which would provide the entertainment portion of the next evening's Centennial Ball.

'Now let me see if I have this straight, Mr Wyndham,' she said, more than a little dazed. 'The first hole starts upstairs, in the corridor outside the upstairs bar—'

'The New Bar, we call it,' club president and board of directors' chairman told her. 'It was installed in 1933. The one downstairs – the Old Bar – has been there since the beginning.'

'Outside the New Bar,' Peg adjusted. 'You stand in front of the coatroom door, from where you have to carom the ball off the elephant-foot umbrella stand and over the threshold into the bar—'

'In one stroke,' Wyndham reminded her. 'Otherwise, there is a two-stroke penalty for every stroke over one.'

'Um, right. Now, once in the bar, players are entitled to one Scotch whisky, courtesy of the house, but are immediately disqualified if they order a second. Then, after putting the ball from the bar into the men's card room . . . Mr Wyndham, I'll probably be sorry I asked, but just out of curiosity, why are they disqualified?'

'For a very good reason, Mrs Fiske,' Wyndham said, his thin lips virtually vanishing in a grimace of distaste. 'It's a rule we've had to put in recently to avoid a repetition of the disgraceful exhibition in which Jerrold Pilkoe took advantage of the rules in existence until then, which generously permitted one to order as many drinks as one wished, as long as one didn't hold up the following pairs. He then proceeded to make a fool of himself by falling down the entire upper flight of the grand staircase, after which he picked himself up and dusted himself off, laughing merrily all the time, and *then* proceeded without pause to fall down the *lower* flight, only this time he broke his wrist in the process. He then had the gall to sue the club for negligence and depraved indifference to human life.' The last words were emphasized with a sharp, disapproving nod that produced an accompanying click of his dentures for good measure. '*That* is why.'

'I see,' Peg said, not knowing what else to say. 'And this happened recently, you said? Last year?'

Wyndham blinked. 'It happened in 1949.'

Peg blinked too. 'I see.'

One couldn't blame him for taking a somewhat longer view of time than she did, being that he was well over twice her age, and she was hardly a dewy maiden. 'I'm ninety-two years of age,' he'd bragged to her before she'd known him five minutes. 'The oldest member of the Royal Mauna Kea.' A moment later he'd amended: 'Well, not counting Babbington, of course. But I'm the oldest member who still has all his marbles.' And then yet a further muttered afterthought. 'Well, most of them.'

She cleared her throat. 'Now, just to move out ahead, the same rule applies to the men's card room and the library, where one whisky only may be ordered . . .'

'And to the smoking room and the ballroom.'

'Right.' It was a wonder any of them could see straight by the time they finished. 'You know, I think maybe I'd better write all this down,' she said, producing a pen and leather-bound notepad from her purse.

At the sight of the notebook, Wyndham held up a knobbly finger and imperiously motioned her to come along. 'No need to write anything down. I've got just the ticket for you. It's right upstairs.'

To her surprise he headed, not for the elevator, but for the broad, gleaming staircase that angled up three sides of the grand foyer. For a frail-looking old gaffer, he was remarkably spry, especially considering that he'd already taken her on a thorough tour of the impressive old clubhouse. Peg was puffing slightly by the time she'd followed him up both flights to the upper floor.

The building's interior was really something to see: a Victorian mansion – a palace, almost – with stucco reliefs on the ceilings, crystal chandeliers, tall, richly sculpted marble fireplaces, and handsome bronze table-top sculptures, mostly of animals either fighting one another or eating one another. There was beautiful, exquisitely finished wood everywhere – mahogany, redwood, Hawaiian koa wood – from the stair-case, to the massive, squared-off support pillars, to the carved, linen-fold wall paneling of some of the smaller rooms.

But beyond all the sumptuousness was a slightly tatty quality: the carpets and rugs were threadbare, the sofa cush-ions had been squashed flat years ago, beyond anyone's ability to re-plump them, and the heavy drapes were faded and moth-eaten. This shabbiness, Peg felt sure, was not the result of lack of money or concern, but of a let's-not-fuss-over-it attitude that she had seen before: part of the 'conspic-uous non-consumption' ethic of the super-rich.

Taken altogether – there was also a broad, lovely flag-stone terrace overlooking the first tee, with an area for casual-dress outdoor dining (in the main dining room, even Bermuda shorts were *verboten*) – it was a clubhouse that any country club would love to have for its own, and no doubt one that brought in megabucks for initiation fees and dues. She was reluctant to ask Wyndham what it cost to join – he would no doubt regard it as a shocking breach of etiquette – but she was pretty sure it took a six-figure check, with substantial monthly dues on top of that. Super-rich, all right.

Wyndham led her into the redwood-paneled library, stop-ping at a leather-bound, atlas-sized tome that lay open on its own stand next to a marble bust of the club's mutton-chop-whiskered patriarch, the great and far-sighted Augustus Cumberland.

'This,' he intoned, indicating the book, 'is the Great Logbook of the Royal Mauna Kea Golf and Country Club. It's been right here since the day the club opened its doors, on February eighth of the year 1905.' He lifted a sheaf of heavy pages to reveal a sheet of four hand-tinted renderings of the building's exterior, from front, back, and each of the two sides.

'The original architectural elevations,' he said proudly. 'My father was the architect, you know. Nathan Wyndham. He was quite well known. I'm sure you've heard of him.'

'Um, uh, of course,' Peg said. 'Nathan Wyndham. My goodness.'

Wyndham ran his hand lovingly, almost greedily, around the fine-grained red-leather margins of the cover. 'Genuine Cordovan leather, made especially in Spain. You don't see this kind of leather any more, I can tell you that.'

No you don't, Peg thought, because in the old days the hide they'd used had come from the rear end of a horse. Nowadays pigskin and goatskin got into the act, coarsening the texture but lowering the price. All things considered, she thought it was better to keep this fact to herself.

On a rack above the logbook was a pen – the dipping kind, not a fountain pen or a ballpoint – and a dented old copper inkwell of the sort she'd thought had gone out of use in about 1811. The book, she could see, was a giant record book with ancient, spidery entries visible on the open page. A second glance told her that, spidery they might be, but ancient they weren't. The last two entries appeared to be for the current day.

Wyndham tapped the volume reverently with his palm. 'It's in here, it's all in here,' he said, as Merlin might have said while tapping his secret book of incantations. He began turning the stiff, parchment-like pages a few at a time, and Peg caught a glimpse of a page of illuminated, meticulously drawn calligraphy, almost like a sheet from a medieval bible. Struck with its beauty, she touched it to stop its turning, and softly read the first few lines aloud.

The Ancient and Honourable Oath
Whose is it? Yours and yours alone.
Why must I seek it? For the Continuance of the
    Brotherhood.
Where must I seek it?

'Why, this is beautiful,' she said. 'Is it some kind of membership ritual?'

But Hamish had brushed her hand out of the way, hastily turned past the page, and gone on flipping. 'Oh, just some old rite from years ago. Decades, really. Ah, here's what we're looking for,' he said, stopping a few dozen pages further on, at a hand-drawn diagram with ample handwritten notations. 'This is our current Indoor Putting Championship course, pretty clearly explained, I think. And here,' he said, turning back a few pages, 'are all the pairings for the last one hundred years, not one single year missed! Not very many of our members play any more, but it's an old tradition and valued for that reason. You can make up the pairings from last year's list. I'd say doing it randomly would suit fine, as long as you don't pair any of the same people again.'

'Pairings?' Peg said, surprised. 'You want me to work up pairings? You don't just choose your own partners?'

'Choose our own partners, did you say?' One tangled eyebrow tipped up and quivered. The red-rimmed, pale-blue eyes underneath reprimanded her. 'And have the same team win every year? Wouldn't be sporting, would it?'

Peg shook her head. 'No . . . no, of course not. What was I thinking?' She cleared her throat again. 'One question, though. I know that many of the members are, er, getting on in years. How will I know . . .' She searched for a delicate way of phrasing it, but gave up. 'How will I know who's, um, around, and who's, ah, not here any more?'

Surprisingly, Wyndham chuckled. 'Well, nobody's croaked this last year, if that's what you're trying to say, knock on wood. Well, nobody but old Sondergard, so I suppose you'd best not include him, heh-heh-heh. Well, I'd better be going, have a tee time coming up and we're pretty strict about tee times. I leave it to you, then, Mrs Fiske. Scramble them up good.'

After he left, Peg went to the library window to look down on the beautifully maintained course below – clearly the club spared no expense for maintenance there – where Wyndham, gnarled and stringy, trotted (well, nearly) to the first tee, where cronies nearly as old as he was waited.

'How old,' she mused, 'do you have to be before a ninety-two-year-old man calls you "old Sondergard"?'

Four

Once, when Graham had been late getting back for dinner from a meeting at the security consulting firm he ran, Lee had spent a pleasant hour browsing among his books in his airy apartment on California's Monterey Peninsula. Without much real interest, she had picked up one on ancient Egypt, and had been unexpectedly caught up in the lively writing. The book was called *Red Land, Black Land*, and in it the author, Barbara Mertz, had memorably described the remarkably sharp border between the fertile black land of the Nile Valley, cultivated for thousands of years, and the empty, sand-blasted desert down which (or rather, up which) it ran from one end of the country to the other.

If Mertz had written a book about the Big Island of Hawaii, Lee thought from her vantage point on the eighteenth green of the Royal Mauna Kea Golf Club, she would have done well to call it *Green Land, Brown Land*. The difference between the Kohala lowlands' brown, lifeless plain of jagged lava fields and the lush landscapes of the golf courses and resorts that were strung out along the coast couldn't have been more stark. You could literally be standing with one foot on a carpet of soft, thick grass so green it hurt your eyes, with palm trees and masses of wonderfully fragrant blossoms – purple, white, orange, pink – everywhere, while the other foot was on a gritty, jumbled moonscape of lava the color of dried blood. If you had eyes on the sides of your head, like a snake or a bird, so that you could see in two different directions at once, you'd never know both eyes were looking at the same island.

Here's to you, Augustus Cumberland, she thought. You had a heck of a lot more imagination than I do. Never in a million years would I have envisioned a cool, green golf course alongside this vast, grim landscape where nothing lived or could live.

Not that Lee's imagination was weak; quite the opposite. That was what was giving her problems right this minute, and why she'd been spending so much time this morning gazing at lava fields in the middle distance, instead of politely following the play of her golf foursome. As a matter of fact, she was working hard *not* to watch her companions, especially around the greens. All three of them were senior – very senior – members of the board of directors. ('Those guys are so old,' Wally had said, 'that when they order three-minute eggs the waiter asks for the money up front.') And while they were remarkably good from the tee and on the fairway – in their primes, they must have been quite something – when it came to the putting green, every last one of them had the 'yips.'

Dreaded as they were, the yips were rarely talked about by pros, and when they were, it was with marked unease, as if the mere talking might cause one to catch a case of them. As near as anybody knew, the yips were caused by muscular tension that affected the small movements of a golfer's hands and wrists, rather than the big, powerful muscles of the torso and legs, so that the sufferer's putting deconstructed in an agony of spasms, jerks and hesitations. And the shorter the putt – the closer to the hole you came – the yippier you got. Great golfers from Sam Snead and Ben Hogan to Tom Watson and Bernhard Langer had been afflicted with the yips, and any professional golfer would go to great lengths not to hear about them, or think about them, or see them in action. Hence all the gazing at the lava fields.

Still, Lee took a chance and glanced back toward the hole – thank God it was the last one – then quickly turned away again, as unobtrusively as she could. There was the board chairman and club president, Hamish Wyndham, whose turn it was to putt. His beaky nose jutting out like a bird of prey's, his brow furrowed above his tangled eyebrows, his entire frame radiating apprehension, he stood as if turned to stone over a ball lying five feet from the hole. Armed with a belly putter that was almost as long as he was (the butt of which was braced against his collarbone instead of his abdomen), he finally started moving again, with all the fluid grace of Frankenstein's monster being jolted into life by a jagged bolt of lightning. Swaying back and forth once, twice, three times (to build up momentum?), he suddenly stabbed at the ball, sending it skidding twenty feet past the hole.

'Too bad,' commiserated Amory Aldrich, a shambling, slow-speaking giant of a man who must once have been a magnificent physical presence. Now age had unfleshed him and bent his back, but even so he stood a good six-foot-three, with hands as big as shovels and feet that must have been size fifteens. With a barely perceptible sigh he stepped resolutely toward his own ball. His lips turned downward. 'My turn,' he said joylessly.

Lee again averted her eyes. Aldrich had what must once have been a decent pendulum putting stroke, but nowadays he fussed with it so much that watching him was like watching a man beating off a swarm of bees. Just to look at him in action made her own hands long to twitch. She waited for what she hoped was long enough, then looked back toward him just in time to see the ball running almost entirely around the rim of the hole before falling into the cup with a triumphant *clunk*. He'd done it!

'Great putt!' she whooped with the rest of them. Aldrich gracefully accepted their congratulations and retrieved his ball with the aid of the suction cup on the end of his putter, a device all three of them wisely used, to avoid bending over.

Evan Bunbury, the only one of them who had more flesh on him than the absolute minimum required to sustain life, was the yippiest of all, but he seemed to accept the afflictions of age with resignation, good humor, and a ready repertoire of jokes about getting old. At the beginning of the round, when Aldrich had greeted him with 'You're looking good, Evan,' he had turned to Lee with a twinkle in his eye. 'People are always saying, "You look good, Evan." Did you know that according to science there are three ages of man? Youth, middle age, and "You're looking good, Evan."' And then he'd dissolved in silent laughter, his ample shoulders jiggling. Lee laughed too, but his two companions merely looked stoically on with the resigned air of men who had heard Evan Bunbury's jokes five or six hundred times too often. After seventeen holes, Lee was beginning to feel the same way. Besides, at eighty, Evan was the youngster of the threesome; there was something that struck Lee as unfeeling about his joking about old age with men a decade older than him.

Bunbury's approach to putting was to sneak up behind his ball, as if pretending he just happened to be in the neighborhood. Then he would quickly take his stance, hoping that the ball wouldn't notice, murmur, 'Here goes nothing,' and take his putter smoothly back. That is, the part in his hands would swing smoothly back, but the part that was on the ground, the part that counted – the club head – would stick behind the ball as if glued to the grass. A moment later it would jerk violently back, violently forward, and the ball would leap ahead – or sideways, or, on one memorable occasion, backwards. Generally it took four or five repetitions before he nailed it.

Lee had no desire to witness any of this for the eighteenth time. Her eyes sought the nearest pile of lava and studied it intently until she heard the ball drop into the cup. That meant it was her turn to putt. Her chip shot from sixty yards had landed only two feet from the hole. Ordinarily, this was as close to a sure thing as anything could be; she could knock it in with one hand, or with her eyes closed. But ordinarily, she didn't spend an entire morning surrounded by yipsters. Keeping her mind a blank, she walked up to the dime she used as a marker, placed her ball in front of it, picked up the dime, and putted out, all pretty much in one casual motion.

Whew! Although the game meant nothing on its own, she'd been anxious for these experienced golfers more than three times her age to see her as a competent professional.

'Ah, to have joints as young as that,' Aldrich said wistfully, watching as she effortlessly stooped to get her ball. 'I believe I once did, but I don't know that I'd swear to it.'

'Oh, I don't know, Amory,' said Bunbury. 'There are certain advantages to having old joints, you know.' He paused expectantly. Another joke was coming, but the other two men refused to cooperate. Lee felt obliged to lend a hand.

'What are they?' she asked dutifully.

'For one thing, no one expects you to run into a burning building,' Bunbury replied, jiggling soundlessly away. 'For another, people don't think you're a hypochondriac any more. For another, your joints are more accurate than the National Weather Service. For another—'

'Come, gentlemen,' Wyndham said, sternly tapping the face of his wristwatch. 'Board meeting beckons.'

'What's on the agenda this time?' Evan Bunbury asked with a sigh. 'Not another ultimatum from the Hooey Mooey Makapooey people?'

'Hui Malu Makuahine Pele,' Aldrich said soberly. 'And I wouldn't joke so cavalierly about them, if I were you.'

Bunbury rolled his eyes. 'Amory, sometimes I wonder about you, I really do.'

In the brief, awkward silence that followed, Lee asked, 'Is that the fringe group that wants the Mana Stone returned?' From their expressions it was clear they were surprised that she knew anything about it, so she added, 'Wally told me about them yesterday.'

A glowering glance between the three men told her that she had made a mistake. Rats, now she'd gone and gotten Wally in trouble with the three senior members of his board for airing matters outsiders weren't supposed to know about. 'I mean, he didn't want to tell me, I guess, but I kept asking him questions, and he was a little dizzy from, um, painkillers and things, I suppose, and, uh . . .'

Aldrich saved her from further blathering. 'The name means "the Society of Mother Pele," Miss Ofsted,' he explained. 'And I would hesitate to call it a fringe group. Their interest in—'

'Well, I wouldn't hesitate to call it hooey,' Bunbury said aggressively, staring up at the taller man.

Aldrich glared right back down at him. 'Evan,' he said solemnly, 'my travels have taken me to many remote and exotic places in the world, and I've seen with my own eyes things that are inexplicable to our limited Western—'

'That's enough!' Wyndham said sharply. 'The answer to your question, Evan, is yes. The club has received another letter. Wally will have it for us at the meeting.'

'Oh, God . . .' Evan began.

'I feel much as you do about these Pele people, Evan,' Wyndham interrupted, 'but this letter is a bit different. Wally read it to me. He'll have it for us at the meeting.'

You mean Wally is already up and around and back to work? she almost exclaimed, but since her last intercession had apparently scraped some shins, she kept it to herself.

'There are also several other administrative matters that need our attention,' Wyndham continued. 'Miss Ofsted, it's been a pleasure and a privilege to play with you.' He tried a courtly bow, making it about halfway.

'I loved it,' Lee said, lying prettily through her teeth. 'Thank you so much. You have a wonderful course here.'

That part, at least, was true.

Five

Wally was wondering about the wisdom of getting back into harness so quickly. What had been his hurry? The board could have taken action (or more likely inaction) on the letter without him, and the rest of the agenda was all administrivia. Why hadn't he taken Cookie's advice and spent his first day back from the hospital at home and in bed? ('They're grown-ups. They functioned before you came, and they'll function after you're gone,' she had said.)

Well, yes, but Cookie had little idea of how unpredictable and capricious these five ill-assorted characters could be. He'd missed a meeting before, and learned after the fact that Hamish had put up a cost-cutting motion to eliminate the position of restaurant manager and add her responsibilities to Wally's, which would have turned his life into absolute hell. The motion had failed, but only by a three-to-two margin. (Evan Bunbury, ever supportive of Hamish, had voted for it too.) That had been the last time he'd been absent from a board meeting, and he wasn't about to chance it again. There was also the added attraction of being the minutes taker. More than once a little deft editing of the minutes had saved them from making public fools of themselves – and of him.

But all that didn't make him any less miserable. His ankle, propped straight out on the leeboard of the wheelchair, throbbed like a sore tooth. The hospital had given him codeine to take home with him, but he'd taken nothing stronger than a couple of ibuprofen tablets an hour before the meeting. He knew better than to be anything less than at his sharpest when he was dealing with the board. And he hated not being

34

up on his feet. The docs had told him that if the swelling stayed down all day they'd put him in a walking cast tomorrow morning, and then he could hobble around on crutches, which he preferred. At least he'd be looking people straight in the eye instead of up at them.

He had gotten to the boardroom early, to give himself a chance to navigate the bulky, unfamiliar wheelchair into the room and up to the oval table in a spot where nobody was likely to bump into his leg. He closed his eyes and collected himself for the ordeal ahead. Board meetings were trials at the best of times, and this was not the best of times.

'Does this look all right, Wally? Give me your honest opinion,' Grace McCulloch inquired in a tone that clearly permitted but one answer.

'Yes, it looks fine,' Wally said on cue. 'They'll love it.'

The object she referred to was a folding table along one wall of the room, on which Grace and a helper had set an attractive lunch buffet – bread and rolls, an artfully arranged platter of cold cuts and cheeses, carrot and celery sticks, coffee, soft drinks, bottled water and fresh, sliced papaya, banana, kiwi, and pineapple – all under tautly stretched plastic.

In truth, he thought, they would by no means love it, although that wouldn't stop them from consuming it. Penurious to a man, they would surely object to the expense of this needless extravagance, and Hamish Wyndham would no doubt lead the grumbling. This, he suspected, was fine with Grace, who was Hamish's sole offspring, having been born Grace Wyndham.

Hamish had once shown Wally a picture of her at twenty, and she had been a beauty. Now, in her late fifties, she'd taken on the looks of her father – leathery and pinch-faced – and was capable of being every bit as disagreeable. Currently a resident of Tucson and lately divorced, she'd come to Hawaii for the week, ostensibly to help out with decorations and such for the Centennial, but Wally was pretty sure she also had another agenda in mind. Hamish Wyndham – stringy, stingy old Hamish, who had once so strenuously resisted the incursions of native Hawaiians into the club – had returned from a weekend trip to Honolulu earlier in the month with a new wife in hand, a quiet, pudding-faced widow of mixed Hawaiian and Haole stock named Sally Mehai Templeton, who happened to be well under half his age.

The marriage had come as an unwelcome shock to the stuffier members of the Royal Mauna Kea, of whom there were many. Kathy, his first wife, had been the offspring of high-society parents; her father was the second-generation owner of the island's biggest macadamia-nut farm. Sally was not only half-Hawaiian, and unprepossessing at that, she had been employed as a home health-care worker, taking care of the aged, when she'd met Hamish. The joke going around was that she'd still be doing the same kind of work, only now she wouldn't be getting any pay for it.

It had surely come as a shock to Grace as well. Wally had no doubt at all that she had come here to have a jaundiced look at her father's new wife and perhaps to let him know, in various 'subtle' ways, just what she thought of this latest senile folly of his.

'And here they come,' Wally said. 'Better whip that plastic wrap off and get your fingers out of the way if you want to keep them.'

Hamish was first through the door, and he wasted no time stepping into character. The buffet table was near the entrance, and for a few seconds he watched the helper, a club kitchen employee, remove the wrap and turn smilingly to him for his approval. She was met instead with a monkey-like grimace of displeasure.

'This feast, is it in the budget?'

The helper was struck speechless. 'It . . . it . . .'

'You can afford it, Dad, believe me,' Grace threw over her shoulder, fussing with the cheese arrangement. 'Bessie, we're going to need some more ice for the drinks.'

'It's not a question of whether *I* can afford it, it's a question of whether the club can afford it.'

'The club can afford it,' Grace told him, still not bothering to look at him.

The homecoming of Grace McCulloch had not been going well, Wally surmised. And indeed, how well could a meeting between a fifty-seven-year-old stepdaughter and a new stepmother fourteen years her junior be expected to go?

'Damn it, Grace,' Hamish rumbled, 'I won't be—'

'I have to go now,' Grace said curtly. 'There's a lot to be done.'

'Now . . . now listen to me, young lady—' But she was already out the door.

Wally, much practiced in calming Hamish down, interceded. 'Actually, there isn't any expense, Hamish. This is all just extra from the lunch we brought in for the decorating committee and the people helping them out. It's already been paid for. The caterers said they could spare it easily.'

Hamish redirected his wrath at Wally. 'Why was it already paid for if it wasn't needed in the first place? Why was it ordered at all?'

But the steam had gone out of him. He was flying on automatic pilot now, expressing his continued and long-standing irritation at the 'exorbitant' extra costs involved in the Centennial. Hamish's approach to club finances, his very attitude to life, was that there should never be additional expenses – for anything, at any time, no matter the rationale. And three of the other four directors agreed with him.

Not that that stopped them heading for the lunch spread the moment they came in and falling on it like a gang of hungry truckers. It had long been a matter of wonder and amusement to Wally that these prodigiously rich old guys reacted to 'free' food the way ravening wolves reacted to a flock of sheep. Evan Bunbury, Amory Aldrich, and beer scion Bernie Gottschalk gingerly carried plastic plates loaded to their extreme limits to their usual seats at the table. Hamish, perhaps constrained by what he had just said, was more delicate at first, taking a little bit of this and a little bit of that, but in the end he too got carried away and came to the table with a heaped plate. How a guy like him could put away the amount he did and still stay so meager was a source of continuing amazement.

The only person to hang back, other than Wally, was the one female member of the board, and the first native Hawaiian ever to serve on it. Lynn Palakahela, who came into the room a few minutes after the others, had in fact been the first full-blooded Hawaiian to be granted membership of the Royal Mauna Kea Golf and Country Club. In 1996, after three consecutive years of placing first in the Hawaii Amateur Stroke Play Championship, she had applied to join. Hamish, feeling – accurately, in Wally's opinion – that she was more interested in making a political and sociological point than in the charms of the club, had led the resistance against her entry, going so far as to blackball her on her first try. He had long ago resigned himself, however grudgingly, to the presence of women in the club, but *kanakas*? That was some-thing else altogether. (This was, of course, well before his recent marriage.) However, when even some mainland news-papers got into the act on her behalf, he and his many supporters had had to back down, and she had been admitted. Now a prominent realtor in the Kohala area, last year she had gotten herself elected to the board, where she continued to tweak the fusty old Victorian mindset of the club and to annoy Hamish at every opportunity.

She started in good form. When Hamish set his plate down on the conference table (with a weighty, audible thud) and said, 'The meeting is called to order,' she replied casually from the buffet, 'Give me a minute, Hamish, I'm trying to see if there aren't a few scraps of food left here. Apparently, the locusts have been in . . . oh, look, a whole quarter slice of Swiss cheese.'

Hamish muttered something.

'And, oh my,' Lynn continued, poking through the plat-ters, 'here's the bottom half of a mini bagel that somebody missed!'

She came to the table with the said items on her plate,

along with a can of 7-Up, and sat down, smiling innocently. The others looked guiltily at their own mounded food, but Wally laughed to himself. He knew that Lynn, one of the very few members with whom he occasionally played golf for pleasure, generally skipped lunch altogether.

'Do you suppose we can start now?' Hamish asked sourly. 'Hand out the letter, Wally.'

'But read it out loud as well, will you?' said Evan Bunbury, who didn't take long getting over his guilt and tucking in. 'I'm old. I can't eat and read at the same time any more.'

Wally complied, sliding copies across the polished walnut table to them and keeping the original for himself. The letter, like the previous ones, was on thick, expensive, cream-colored paper, neatly written (not typed or computer-produced) in jet-black ink, in tiny, old-fashioned capital letters. He read aloud from it:

'"Pele has waited long enough. Her patience is at an end. The time is growing near. The Mana Stone MUST be returned to mighty Mauna Kea without delay. If you fail to relinquish this sacred stone, her anger will be terrible, and the dreadful prediction of the Fourth Chant of the First Book of the Night World will be fulfilled.

'"Thus will it be done. Sand, ashes, and burning stones will spew from the Pit into a column of fire standing straight up. The great mountains of Mauna Kea and Mauna Loa will be as nothing beneath it. The people far away on Kauai will tremble with awe at this wonderful column with fire glowing and blazing to its very top. But in Kohala all will be wailing and grief. Men, women, and infants will die. Where now stand the great and wealthy palaces of the oppressors will be only death and desolation, lava fire and smoke. And no sacrifice of pigs or other offering can halt this, only the return of the Mana Stone to its father, the mountain.

'"We of Hui Malu Makuahine Pele cannot permit this

to occur. If the Stone is not quickly returned to its father, we will take matters into our own hands. Our retaliation will be swift and without mercy, and will continue until the Stone is secure. What is the life of one or two *malihini* compared to such a catastrophe?"'

'That's it.' Wally put the paper down and waited. For a moment there was nothing but steady chomping, and then Hamish said: 'Comments?'

'Yes,' Evan said. 'I thought the mountain was its mother.'

Hamish looked at him. 'What?'

'It said "its *father* the mountain." The last letter said it was its *mother* the mountain. So which is it, that's what I want to know.'

Hamish continued to stare irritably at him. 'We're not here to discuss the damn thing's parentage, Evan. We're here to discuss what to do about this letter, if anything. Do you have anything serious to offer?'

Hamish's and Evan's relationship went back farther than any other that Wally knew about. They were, as another old member had once said to him, the Damon and Pythias of the club. (Wally thought Mutt and Jeff would have been closer to the mark, given their appearances.) Their fathers had owned nearby sugar plantations (Hamish's architect-dad Nathan had bought his and moved to Hawaii after falling in love with the clubhouse he'd designed; the Bunburys went back a couple of generations), and although Evan was Hamish's junior by a dozen years, the two had become close in the 1930s – close in the sense that Hamish looked out for Evan, and Evan adored his dashing, handsome, older friend. When Hamish had won the Mauna Kea Men's Championship at the age of twenty-two, the ten-year-old's adoration had turned to hero worship. Evan, following in his idol's footsteps, had won a club championship of his own not so many years afterward, and that had cemented their friendship and put them on a more even footing. Later, they had even fallen in love with the same girl, so the well-known story went – the famously beautiful Kathy Mahnerd. But with Evan a fat and pimply eighteen, five years her junior, and Hamish a mature and manly thirty, there was no contest. Hamish had married her in 1943 and Evan, a romantic through and through (hard to believe now!), had joined the Navy and gone off to war with his broken heart.

As they always do, however, the broken heart apparently mended. Evan had eventually married (and divorced) since then, and his friendship with Hamish was still strong, although they had long ago established a grumpy, joshing, old-guy's way of dealing with each other. Both men had sold their sugar interests decades before. They now lived, and apparently lived very well, on income from their investments.

'Put it in the round file,' Evan said predictably, in response to Hamish's question. 'Why is it any different from the last few we've gotten?'

'Well, no,' Amory Aldrich said, slowly masticating, 'this one's different, all right. It's the first time there's been a direct threat like that. Just read those last few sentences again. They've never said anything like that before. Unless I'm missing something, they're talking about killing people. Us, to be exact.'

Evan shrugged his unconcern and went back to lathering mustard on the inside of a split roll, preparatory to inserting a stack of ham slices. 'My goodness, I'm just too scared to speak,' he said.

'I have to agree with Evan,' said Lynn. 'It's ridiculous. It's more of the same schoolboy nonsense. What's the Fourth Chant of the First Book of the Whatever supposed to be? It's not part of any Hawaiian mythology I ever heard of, and even if it was, are we really supposed to quail at the mention of Pele?'

The athletic, hard-bodied, bluntly outspoken Lynn was an interesting case, Wally thought. On the one hand, she was a vigorous proponent of the extreme nativist movement that sought to return governing power to Hawaiians, by which she didn't mean second- or third- or fifth-generation

41

Hawaiians whose ancestors immigrated from Japan, or China, or the United States, but to 'true' Hawaiians – those who could trace their roots back 2,000 years to the original Polynesian settlers. On the other hand, she had nothing but contempt for traditional Hawaiian culture and religion, considering them a yoke around the neck of the native people. On either hand, she had no hesitation about expressing her views, a trait that got a lot of people's hackles up. Hamish wasn't the only one she annoyed. Personally, Wally thought she was a terrific addition to the board. Not that she was any less wacky than the rest, just wacky in a different way.

'What does *malihini* mean, Lynn?' Amory asked. 'Foreigners? Americans?'

She nodded. 'Essentially. Strangers, to be exact.'

'Us, as Amory has already pointed out,' said Evan, swallowing a chunk of ham sandwich. 'Well, I'm petrified, just petrified.'

'Go ahead and joke about it,' Amory said, chewing. 'But I tell you here and now, these myths and legends don't last for thousands of years because there's no basis to them.' He leaned forward, his massive brow lowered, and gestured darkly with a carrot stick. '"There are more things in heaven and earth, Horatio, than are dreamt of in your philosophy."'

'I doubt if Shakespeare had Mother Pele in mind,' Lynn said drily.

'What do you think, Bernie?' Hamish asked, turning to a rumpled, balding, coarse-featured man with what he must have thought was a genial and inquisitive smile.

Bernhard Gottschalk, the man addressed, was the board's newest and youngest member, a blunt, short-spoken businessman of forty-five. He had outraged many in the club by his vulgar and unprecedented tactic of bringing in a professional political consultant to manage his election campaign, but although it had made him some enemies, it had also won him the seat. Why he wanted it at all was a mystery to many, because he showed little interest in club affairs and rarely had anything of substance to contribute.

It wasn't a mystery to Wally, however. Bernie wanted the seat for the same reason he had applied for club membership in the first place: to impress and enlarge his circle of business contacts. Bernie, who had inherited a fortune as the inheritor of a brewery empire (Gottschalk's Grand Reserve Lager), was now enlarging that fortune as one of Hawaii's most spectacularly successful venture capitalists. In all probability, he was the richest member of the board, and possibly of the club itself.

Nonetheless, Bernie too had failed in his first try for membership, blackballed by – who else? – Hamish, the club's most energetic blackballer, who found Bernie's social credentials not all they might have been. ('A family brewery, for God's sake! And . . .' (Shudder) 'Just consider the man *himself*! Those two-dollar cigars!')

But Bernie had found allies and Hamish had withdrawn his objections, publicly if not privately. Now Bernie, like Lynn, had elevated himself to the august ranks of the board of directors, and Hamish, who could face reality if it hit him in the face hard enough, had reluctantly come to see that he was that most valuable of colleagues: the swing vote. There were certain issues on which the other four members were likely to deadlock – namely the liberalizing of the course dress code and the democratization of membership rules, which Lynn and Amory consistently voted for and Evan and Hamish equally consistently voted against. Bernie, with no strong feelings either way, sometimes went with one pair, sometimes with the other. True, he had probably come down more often on Lynn and Amory's side, but that gave Hamish all the more reason to cultivate him.

Bernie, caught by Hamish's question in the middle of a mouthful of roast beef and cheese, shrugged his unconcern.

'No, we'd really like to know,' Hamish persisted with a skeletal smile. His continuing effort to be ingratiating made Wally's teeth ache. 'Your views are very important here.'

Another shrug, during which the food went down. 'OK, then, if you want my opinion, I don't see why we just don't take the damn stone off the cup and dump it on the mountain to get them off our backs. We could make a big show out of it. Be good publicity, and we'd still have the cup, wouldn't we?'

The others just looked at him. It was Lynn who spoke. 'But we don't *have* the cup, Bernie. That's the problem.'

Bernie was already concentrating on building his second sandwich. 'Yeah, that's a point,' he agreed amiably.

It wasn't, Wally thought, that he was dumb. He just didn't give a damn.

'I move we simply ignore it,' said Evan, who had finished his lunch and was drumming his fingers on the table.

'Second,' said Lynn.

'All in favor—' began Hamish.

'Can I make a suggestion?' Wally interrupted as politely as he could. 'Are you sure you don't want to consider at least turning the letter over to the police?'

'I don't think we want the cops involved,' Bernie said. 'That's not the kind of publicity we need.'

'I know, but as Amory said, there's an out-and-out threat here.'

Hamish sniffed. 'Hardly one to take seriously.'

'But who knows, if we gave the police a chance, they might actually catch some of those damn diggers.'

'And that's another thing,' Hamish said, leveling a warning finger at Wally. '*You* stay away from those diggers too. These ridiculous and unnecessary "accidents" of yours are going to result in an increase in our insurance premiums, you'll see.'

'But the course—'

'You and the groundskeepers can repair the course just fine. This sort of thing is a fad. It's come and gone before, and it will pass again. Turf, as I have often said before, is a renewable resource.'

Wally had heard this before. He held up his hands in defeat. 'Whatever you say. I only work here, what do I know?'

Hamish crisply nodded his agreement. 'And now, if there's nothing else—'

'I have something,' Lynn said bluntly. 'These Hui Malu Makuahine people aren't the only ones with ignorant superstitions. Don't you think the Centennial – our hundredth anniversary—'

Wally saw Hamish stiffen at the word 'our.' As far as he was concerned, she might have bulled her way into becoming a member, but that didn't give her proprietary rights.

'—would be an excellent time for getting rid of our own ludicrous, antiquated mumbo-jumbo? Start the second hundred years with a clean slate? Drag ourselves into the twentieth century, at any rate, even if we're not quite ready for the twenty-first.'

Hamish tilted his head back and peered down his aristocratic nose at her. 'I have no idea to what you're referring.'

But he did, Wally knew, and so did everyone else. This was hardly the first time Lynn had voiced her contempt for the most venerable, if unfathomable, practice of the club. She was referring to the Ancient and Honourable Oath, administered in the form of a spooky, supposedly secret catechism to new members as a part of their initiation.

'I'm talking about that ridiculous oath,' she said. 'It's a positive embarrassment, every bit as stupid as those letters.'

'You know, I have to say that it really is a little silly,' Amory agreed in his slow, patient way. 'A little old-fashioned for the times. People used to enjoy the hocus-pocus of it, but now I'm not so sure any more. Perhaps it *is* time to retire it.'

'You bet,' Bernie agreed. 'It's a load of crap.'

'But it's a tradition,' Evan said sternly. 'It goes back to . . . what, 1910?'

'1908,' Hamish said.

'It could go back to 1508 and it'd still be a load of crap,' said Bernie. 'Nobody knows what it means – if it ever meant anything.'

'It is not . . . *crap*,' Hamish snapped, the ligaments in his neck popping. 'Every line, every word, is filled with meaning. In my day, initiates had to deduce for themselves what the words signified and then actually *perform* the ritual, not merely memorize the answers. We haven't done that for more than sixty years now—'

'Well, why not?' Bernie demanded. 'I mean, if it's so "filled with meaning" . . .'

Hamish talked right over him. 'But we maintain the oath, as Evan says, because this is a club that values tradition.'

'Tradition,' Lynn said cuttingly, 'the opiate of the people.'

'Tradition?' Bernie repeated with an incredulous grunt. 'That's why we keep doing it, even if nobody knows why we keep doing it?'

'*I* know,' Hamish said. He was finding it increasingly difficult to remain civil to Bernie.

'Okay, *you* know. And what happens after you kick off? Then nobody at all will know. It's dumb. I mean . . .' He wanted to say more, but looks from Amory and Evan told him he'd overstepped and he fell silent. This was not a group in which mention of 'kicking off' was good form.

Hamish looked down at the wreckage of his lunch and sighed. 'You know, you're quite right, Bernie,' he said reasonably, taking everyone by surprise. 'I have an idea.' His expression shifted to one of relative merriment, something not often seen on his face. 'I'll tell you what. Why don't I explain the whole thing tonight – to everyone? It's about time, I suppose. I'll walk the entire crowd through it. We can make it part of the celebration. That'd be fitting, wouldn't it? Don't tell anyone. It'll be my little surprise.'

Bernie and the others were so amazed they couldn't say anything.

It fell to Wally to say it for them. 'I'll be damned,' he said softly.

Six

'No, I'm sorry, sir,' Peg said pleasantly. 'We can't count that as a two. The ball has to go *under* the foot stool before it strikes the grandfather clock.'

The young man with the putter in his right hand (and a double margarita in his left) frowned at her. Like many of the people there, he was in evening dress, his neck adorned with a red-white-and-blue silk ribbon from which hung a handsome pewter medallion with palm trees and mountains in low relief, and his name embossed around the rim – the symbol of his membership in the Royal Mauna Kea. 'It does? I thought it just had to come within three feet of the foot stool.'

'No, that's the final hole you're thinking of, where it has to come within three feet of the Chinese urn before striking the right-hand torchère.'

The young man looked skeptical. 'Are you sure about that?'

'Yes, I am,' said Peg, and she was. It was her nature to take seriously any job she took on, and she'd studied the crazy rules until she could say them by heart if required.

'I don't think that's the way it worked last year.'

But older and wiser heads among fellow players and a 'gallery' of onlookers prevailed, firmly backing Peg. 'Just shut up and hit the ball again, Stanley,' he was told wearily by his elders. Which he did.

'Now then, hole fourteen,' said Peg. 'The ball is to be placed at least three inches behind the top step of the landing of the main staircase and struck so that it falls to the bottom, missing no more than six steps in the process. If more than six steps are missed, or the ball does not reach the bottom of the lower flight, it is to be struck again and a one-stroke penalty invoked. Once at the bottom of the stairs, the ball is to be hit, following any trajectory chosen, into the copper spittoon—'

'Eww, gross,' a teenaged voice whined.

'—that has been placed on its side, with its bottom flush against the first wooden column in the Old Bar. Par is four. Are there any questions?'

'We call it the grand staircase, not the main staircase,' an older woman grumbled.

'I beg your pardon,' Peg said, managing to smile while trying not to grit her teeth. 'Ladies and gentlemen, shall we proceed to the grand staircase?'

I just hope, she thought, *that Lee is making good use of the time I've given her with Graham. This is even dumber than I bargained for.*

Seven

The splendid cup, which had seen no light for more than sixty years, stood in its paneled recess, the silver softly gleaming, the traceries of faceted rubies and diamonds glittering and winking like stars. Only the strange, primitively carved lava stone on its bed of white onyx failed to reflect the light, seeming instead to absorb it like some black, underground lake.

Standing before the cup, alone in the elegant, high-ceilinged room, erect and resplendent in black tie and cummerbund, was an old man, his white head bowed, the tips of his skeletal fingers gently touching the medallion that hung from his neck on its silken ribbon. It had been decades – half-a-century, or perhaps more – since tears had last shone on his cheeks, but there they were now, yellow and thick, sliding down the time-etched furrows in his face.

What a long, long time it had been since he, or anyone else, had gazed on the cup, and what a lot had happened since then. A whole life lived, almost to its end. A whole new world now, and none of it to his liking. But wasn't that what old men always said? That the world of their youth had been golden, and good, and lit with promise? That those who came later had not valued what had been earned at such cost and then bequeathed to them? That they had tossed it away so carelessly that the bright hopes of the past, the orderliness, the *rightness* of the world as it had been, had been lost beyond redemption?

Yes, that was what old men always said, and he thought now that it was probably always true. But to rail against it

49

made no sense any more. His world no longer existed, except in the shadows of his own mind and the minds of the few like him that were still left. It was *their* world now, the others', and he was glad he'd finally decided to take the step he was about to take. It was time. It was past time.

As he reached a trembling hand toward the cup to gently caress its curving silver contours – as smooth as a woman's shoulder, he thought; how was it that silver could feel so much like velvet? – he became aware that the door to the room had opened. He spun around. What little color had been in his face drained away. His left leg, subject to nervous spasms, now jerked violently.

'I can explain . . .' he began.

Eight

What a pleasure it was just to be able to sit there and look at him to her heart's content. Clear, intelligent blue eyes (that could make her shiver when they looked so suddenly and deeply into her own). Sandy, neatly cropped hair. Neat, almost military mustache a shade lighter than his hair. Firmness and competence written all over that square-jawed face of his, but an elusive, intangible kindness visible there as well. And wit. And warmth. And gentleness.

She smiled to herself. That was an awful lot to read in an immobile face, especially one that wasn't looking at you. She and Graham had snared a table to themselves in a corner of the ballroom, and were sipping champagne and relaxedly taking in the scene, content and happy in each other's company. Mercifully, from Lee's perspective, none of the indoor putting holes ran through the ballroom, which was exactly why she'd chosen it to spend her first relatively private hour in a month with Graham, who had arrived not much more than an hour earlier. She wasn't about to risk compromising his new appreciation of the weighty import of golf with scenes of half-soused oldsters with too much money and time on their hands hitting balls around potted rubber plants and bouncing them off elephant-foot umbrella stands. (In locating a safe place for them to sit, she had earned no points with Hamish Wyndham by asking him, in all innocence, if the 'silly putting' course ran through the ballroom. 'I am unfamiliar with the "silly putting course" of which you speak,' he had replied with a wintry glare. 'If, however, you are referring to the club indoor putting championship course, it does not. Good evening.')

To be truthful she was curious about how it was going under Peg's capable direction, but that could wait until sometime tomorrow, when she had Peg to herself. Graham's conversion from the 'golf-is-an-inherently-ridiculous-pastime-played-by-people-in-funny-clothes-who-do-a-lot-of-cussing-and-throwing-of-clubs-over-the-most-trivial-circums tances-imaginable' school of thought was too recent to take any chances of a possible setback. The less he heard about the indoor putting, the better.

The crowd in the ballroom was colorful and noisy – there were two temporary bars set up, one at either end – and it could have been a formal occasion anywhere, for any sort of upscale event; charity ball, awards ceremony, conference banquet. The club members were a bit on the elderly side, perhaps, but in their evening dress, and bemedalled with their medallions, they looked refined, attractive, and intelligent. Which, after all, they no doubt were, by and large. This pleased her. She knew that Graham's highly successful security consulting work involved a fair amount of jet-setting that placed him in sophisticated and high-level environments, and it was important to her that he see that she could be comfortable in them as well, even if not exactly accustomed to them.

When she turned back to him she found him staring hard at her – studying her, really – with the faintest of smiles playing about the corners of his mouth; just enough to put an adorable dimple on either side.

'What?' she asked, knowing the blood had risen to her cheeks.

'Just taking in the view,' he said.

'And?'

'And what?'

'What's the verdict?'

'What's the verdict? You want to know what I'm thinking?'

She nodded.

The smile disappeared. Continuing to study her, but in a

sober, meditative way now, he rotated the champagne flute, casting sloshing, transparent reflections on to the tablecloth. She started to feel a little uneasy.

'What I'm thinking,' he said, slowly and earnestly, 'is what a pleasure it is just to be able to sit here and look at you to my heart's content.'

She surprised him by bursting out laughing.

'What's funny?'

'I'll tell you sometime. I love you.'

'You'd better love me. I'm counting on it. That's your pal Wally over there, isn't it? I think he's been trying to get your attention.' He gestured toward a grouping that surrounded a wing chair in which Wally sat rather regally, obviously in the middle of one of his shaggy-dog stories. He had somehow gotten himself into it from his wheelchair, which was pulled up alongside.

Lee got up. 'Okay, let's go over there. I'd like for you to meet him anyway. He is probably the second-most-important man in my life.'

Graham finished his wine and stood up too. '*Your* life? What about mine? If he hadn't been there to teach you, you'd never have learned how to play golf, which means you wouldn't have become a pro, which means you'd never have shown up for the Pacific-Western Tournament, which means I'd never have met you.' He knocked on the wooden table. 'And I owe it all to him.'

In a way, it was all true. It had been three years ago. Lee had been a hungry freshman on the Women's Professional Golf League circuit, and she'd driven from Sacramento with three other low-ranking, low-earning 'rabbits' to the Monterey Peninsula for the tournament. She'd had her first decent outing, earning her expenses and then some, but, more important, she'd crossed paths with a good-looking, good-natured young Carmel police lieutenant named Graham Sheldon and her life hadn't been the same since. Neither had his.

Things had changed for them both quite a bit since then.

Lee was now a well-regarded pro, especially since the Stewart Cup, and Graham had quit police work to start up a security consulting firm that now had three full-time employees and a slew of part-timers, and kept him on a busy international schedule. Their strange, hectic professions – especially Lee's – had been the cause of some ups and downs in their relationship.

'Well, that's one way of looking at it, all right,' she said, taking his hand and skirting the crowded dance floor where several couples of advanced age were doing what appeared to be a foxtrot, despite the fact that the five-man orchestra on the dais was playing a tango. Maybe they weren't so sophisticated after all. 'I guess I owe him even more than I realized.'

'So the dog says, "Don't ask me, ask my monkey,"' Wally was saying as they approached, at which the people around him laughed, some appreciatively and some confusedly, then wandered off when they saw his attention shift to Lee.

'Lee, babe,' Wally said, holding up a hand to her when they reached his side. 'Where the hell is Hamish? Have you seen him?'

'Not for a while. Why? Would you like me to find him for you?'

'The thing is, he was going to walk everybody through that old initiation thing at seven o'clock, and it's five after now. People are starting to wander into the dining room, so if he's gonna do it, now's the time. If he puts it off till after dinner, half of his audience will be asleep. So, yeah, if you could find him and remind him, that'd be good. If he really wants to do it.'

Lee nodded. Wally had told her earlier that Hamish would be explaining the ritual, and she was quite interested herself. 'Sure, but I think the silly putt – the indoor putting championship is still going on, isn't it?'

Wally laughed. 'You got it right the first time, kid. But anyway, I understand Peg's already got them on the eighteenth hole right now – she really moves 'em along, doesn't she? – so it's time.'

'Okay, I'll get him. Wally, this is my fiancé, Graham Sheldon. I've wanted you two to meet for a long time.'

Wally reached up to offer a hand. 'Hey, I've heard all about you.'

'Same here,' said Graham. 'And all good things.'

'Pull over a chair, why don't you?' Wally said. 'Let me tell you what you're getting into, marrying this kid.'

'Uh-oh,' Lee said as Graham complied. 'Maybe this isn't such a good idea.'

'First of all,' Wally said, 'you may have noticed, she has a mind of her own. To put it mildly. She talks back.'

'You know, now that you mention it, I do believe I may have noticed something along those lines, yes.'

Lee folded her arms. 'Now listen, you two—'

'Are you still here?' Wally said, looking up. 'I thought you were going to find Hamish. Come on, make yourself useful. Give your poor old gimpy teacher a hand. Beat it.'

'I wouldn't believe a word he says,' Lee told Graham as she left. 'The man is a well-known compulsive liar.'

There were about a hundred people in the ballroom, so it took a few minutes to see whether or not Hamish was among them. He wasn't. That probably meant he was still with Peg's indoor putting group (although she thought she remembered Peg's saying that he hadn't intended to join in), or in one of the bars. She'd seen him earlier at the entrance to the upstairs bar – or the New Bar, as they called it – so that was where she headed.

No Hamish. But Amory Archer was there with Evan Bunbury and another board member, Bernie Gottschalk, and they told her that Hamish had somewhat distractedly wandered off half an hour earlier saying he'd left his bifocals in his car. They hadn't seen him since.

So back downstairs and outside she went. The parking lot was full – mostly BMWs, Lexuses, Mercedes, with an occasional Jaguar – but the sun hadn't yet set, so it was easy to cruise down the parking lanes and satisfy herself that Hamish wasn't out there. The downstairs bar, the Old Bar, was next. No Hamish. And no Hamish in the Grand Foyer, the dining room, or the kitchen, where someone suggested he might be pursuing one of his favorite activities: persecuting the help. By now she was beginning to get a little concerned. He might have gone to one of the restrooms, of course, but why hadn't he reappeared by now? Upstairs once again, she began opening the doors to the rooms along the corridor, each with a nameplate announcing its function. Three rooms so far: a men's card room, a private dining room, and a well-stocked library, all empty.

'Are you looking for my father?'

The questioner, or rather the demander, was a compact, tight-lipped woman in her fifties, who startled Lee as she closed the double doors to the library.

'Your father?'

'I'm Grace McCulloch. My father is Hamish Wyndham.' They continued walking down the corridor toward the next door together.

'Oh, how do you do? Yes, I was. Do you know where he went?'

'No, I don't. I was hoping you had some idea. The man can be so infuriating sometimes. Without a word to anybody—'

The door Lee was reaching for – 'Christopher Porthmellon Billiards Room' said the plaque – jerked open on its own. She immediately recognized the woman standing in the doorway: Lynn Palakahela, one of Hawaii's finest amateur golfers and a member of the club's board, her hard, athlete's body looking out of place in a bare-armed evening gown. Lee, who had been looking forward to meeting her, put out her hand.

'You're Lynn Palakahela. I'm Lee Ofsted . . .'

But Lynn seemed not to hear her, not even to see her. Gray-faced and stunned, she stared right through Lee and Grace. 'Oh, my God,' she murmured. 'In there . . .'

Something in the vicinity of Lee's stomach shifted and sank. She knew, as surely as if she'd just come from the room herself, what she was about to hear.

Grace seemed to know as well. A soft 'Oh, no,' came from her lips, somewhere between a whisper and a whimper.

Lynn appeared to become aware of them suddenly. Lee could actually see her eyes focus, the black pools of her pupils sharpening and contracting like twin camera lenses. Whether or not she recognized Grace was impossible to tell.

'In there . . .' she said again, her voice just a little stronger, but still somehow far away. 'In there . . . it's . . .'

Hamish Wyndham, Lee's inner voice said.

'Hamish,' said Lynn, and then reached out and enfolded a stunned Grace in her sinewy, bronzed arms. 'Your father. He's . . . he's had an accident. Oh, Grace, I'm so sorry.'

It was indeed Hamish Wyndham, or rather that which had once been Hamish Wyndham. That he was no longer living was obvious from twenty feet away. He lay on his back, not far from the fireplace, at the foot of one of the room's two massive pool tables, spindly legs splayed, arms awry, scrawny neck twisted at an unnatural angle, so that his dulled, half-open eyes seemed to stare directly at them. Scrawny in life, he was yet more shrunken in death, an ancient, wizened doll-man, pathetic in a tuxedo that might once have fit but was now two sizes too large for him. Even his blood, soaking blackly into the saffron carpet under his head and staining his white shirt front, seemed meager and exhausted.

Grace made a motion as if to go to him, but Lynn held her. 'Don't,' she said gently, patting her shoulder. Grace was easy to convince. She permitted herself to be led back into the corridor. Lynn gently closed the door behind them.

'I'll stay with her,' she said to Lee. 'Can you go and find a doctor? Do you know Amory Aldrich? He was a doctor. I think he's—'

Lee nodded. 'I know where he is. I'll get him.'

She would get him, yes, but neither Amory Aldrich nor

any other doctor was going to do Hamish much good, she thought. The awful, blood-matted gouge in Hamish's fragile skull made it clear that what had happened to him was more in Graham's line of work than Amory Aldrich's.

Not that Graham would be able to do Hamish much good either.

Amory was just where Lee had left him, spinning tall tales in the New Bar with Evan Bunbury and Bernie Gottschalk. She quickly told him what had happened – leaving him pop-eyed and murmuring, 'Oh, my Lord,' as he got shakily to his feet – and ran downstairs to the ballroom to find Graham, who was still talking to Wally. Thirty seconds later, with Lee on his heels, Graham burst into the billiards room, the door to which was now wide open. Amory was kneeling beside Hamish, searching for a pulse in Hamish's neck. Bernie and Evan were in the room too, Evan on his knees next to Amory, Bernie leaning over them, his medallion dangling. Both of them looked sick. Word had spread quickly. There were three or four other people in the room, keeping well clear of the body, and outside a knot of onlookers, curious but disinclined to enter, stood in the corridor peering over each others' shoulders.

'Move away from the body, please, sir,' Graham called from the doorway.

Amory started and looked up. He had gotten blood on the sleeves of his white dinner jacket. 'I'm a doctor. I'm afraid this man is dead. I suggest—'

'Sir, will you move away from the body, please? Just stand up and come this way. Don't touch anything else. You two gentlemen do the same,' he told Evan and Bernie.

Blinking, Amory unfolded his long body and obeyed. Evan and Bernie looked at each other uncertainly, appeared for a moment as if they were about to object, then docilely complied as well. All three of them came toward Graham, who hadn't moved from the door.

'Don't touch anything!' he said sharply when Evan rested

a hand for support on the nearest pool table. Evan jerked his hand back as if he'd put it on a hot barbecue grill.

'Everybody else out of the room too,' Graham told the other three or four who had ventured in. 'You,' he said to one of them. 'I want the names of everybody who's entered this room, yours included. You have something to write with?'

The man – a hefty forty-year-old with a scarred, beefy face – responded with a nervous cough and a mute, meek nod, and reached into his inside jacket pocket for a pen.

Lee had seen Graham in police-officer-in-command mode once before. Now, as then, she was amazed at how this easy-going, funny, pleasant man could transform himself into a source of power and authority that cowed just about anybody he came across.

He stepped back out of the way to let them out then closed the door, never having gone beyond the doorsill himself.

'This room is off limits as of now,' he barked. 'No one is to enter it, or come near it. No one is to leave the building under any circumstances, until the police arrive.' He made a herding motion toward the stairs. 'All right, let's get downstairs now. Everyone will wait in the ballroom, please.'

'Who the hell is this guy supposed to be?' Lee heard one annoyed male voice mutter, but she noted that he prudently kept it to a whisper, and that no one answered him.

Nine

Detective Sergeant Milt Fukuda of the West Hawaii Criminal Investigation Section, Kohala Branch, was not so easily cowed by Graham, nor by anyone else. A small, supple, wiry man in his fifties whose bemused, self-confident air and narrowed eyes said he had pretty much seen it all, he had arrived moments before in a dusty, unmarked Honda, and Graham had greeted him on the front steps of the veranda.

'The immediate area's been cleared and secured, Sergeant,' Graham was telling him, while Fukuda, wearing a New York Mets baseball cap and chewing gum, gazed inscrutably back at him with eyelids half lowered. 'And we have the names of everyone who entered after the body was found. Since then, no one's been allowed to enter the room or the building, other than your CSI team and a couple of uniforms, who got here a few minutes ago and have already started taking names and addresses. No one's been allowed to leave the building either, of course . . .' He stopped when he realized Fukuda didn't seem to be paying a whole lot of attention.

A couple of beats passed while Fukuda's eyes wandered over the clubhouse façade and then back to Graham, none too kindly. 'So who are you supposed to be again?' he asked, cracking his gum.

Graham knew what his problem was. To report the finding of Hamish's body, Graham had very properly called 911. Then, because he knew first hand the importance of getting the crime-scene team and the police pathologist there as quickly as possible, before evidence began deteriorating, he had violated protocol by calling the police department directly, then assaulted it further by demanding to speak with a homicide detective. It had been Fukuda who had picked up the phone from the duty officer, and he had been a little hard to convince at first, and a little annoyed as well. Apparently, he still was.

'Look, Sergeant,' Graham said, a bit peeved himself, 'sorry about not going through the proper channels, but we had a pretty obvious case of capital homicide here, and I just didn't see the point of going through the first-officer-on-the-scene routine and all the rest of it. I figured the sooner we got an experienced homicide detail on to it the better.'

'Uh-huh,' Fukuda said. 'So who are you supposed to be again?'

For a detective, Graham thought, he didn't seem to be in much of a hurry to get to the scene of the crime.

'I'm Graham Sheldon. I'm a security consultant—'

'Oh, a security consultant.'

Graham was all too familar with that tone. To most policemen the words 'security consultant' translated to 'rent-a-cop,' which was close to the very bottom of the law enforcement food chain, one level above private investigator.

'I used to be a lieutenant on the Carmel, California police force,' Graham told him crisply. 'Before that, I was a homicide detective in Oakland.'

For the first time, Graham had Fukuda's full attention. 'In Oakland? You've seen your share of murders, then. That's why you talk the talk.'

'Well, yes, I guess—'

He was interrupted by the arrival of a rotund, wheezy man smoking a stubby, unappetizingly well-chewed cigar and carrying a black medical satchel. He nodded at Fukuda. 'Hello, Milt,' he said breathily. 'Who would have thought – murder at the Royal Mauna Kea. My, my, what's this world coming to? Where's it all going to end, do you suppose?'

'Graham Sheldon, this is Sam Kierzek, our coroner. Well, forensic pathologist, really.'

'Well, anatomical pathologist,' Kierzek said. 'At Kona Hospital. I just do this kind of thing part-time because it's nice to look at the occasional body that isn't sick.'

'No, just dead,' said Fukuda.

'That's true,' Kierzek agreed. 'Dead. But except for that, healthy. Usually.' Using forefinger and thumb, he removed the cigar stub from his mouth with surprising delicacy, like a dandy picking up a teacup, and dropped it into an aluminum, freestanding ashtray on the veranda, beside the entrance door. 'So, let's get started.'

'Okay, Graham, lead the way,' Fukuda said, and when they had gone upstairs and arrived at the door of the billiards room and Graham had hung back, he added casually: 'Oh, hell, why don't you come on in too? I can always use another experienced head. You think you still remember how to behave around a crime scene?'

'I'll do my best,' Graham said, pleased. He'd never lost his taste for police work. 'Got any tips for me?'

Fukuda thought about it. Gum cracked. 'It's probably better if you don't step in the blood,' he said.

'Well, it's not exactly rocket science,' Kierzek said, pushing himself to his feet with a weary grunt, stripping off his disposable gloves, and brushing off the knees of his trousers. 'Cause of death should be pretty obvious, even to a simple police officer such as yourself,' he threw out of the side of his mouth at Fukuda.

'Crushing blunt-force trauma of the skull?'

'Oh, you *did* notice!'

The corners of Fukuda's mouth curled down. 'That's hilarious, Doc. What else?'

'Come on, let's get out of here, give your minions room to work,' Kierzek said, indicating the CSI technicians: a woman photographer and two plastic-gloved men who were moving systematically over the area with painful slowness, picking up snippets of this and that and putting them in envelopes and tiny vials. 'He can be moved whenever you want. I'll do the autopsy tomorrow.'

They started to move away, but after just a step Fukuda stopped, peering down at the rim of the pool table. 'What do you make of this?'

He was referring to a narrow dent smashed into the rim and apparently freshly made. The others looked, shook their heads, shrugged, and after a moment continued on into the room across the corridor – the men's card room – and sat down at one of the tables. Kierzek took his time lighting up what Graham believed was called a Churchill: a stogie of monumental proportions.

'Jesus, those things stink,' Fukuda said, screwing up his face against the cloud of smoke. He was still wearing his baseball cap, still cracking his gum. 'I don't know how you do it.'

'You're in no position to complain, Fukuda. I learned to smoke them working for you people, you know. You're the one who told me: nothing like a good cigar to cut the smell of corpse that's been lying around for a while.'

'A *good* cigar, I said.'

'I beg your pardon. This little baby set me back seventy-five cents.'

'What is that, a nickel an inch? At least have some consideration for the rest of us. Breathing second-hand smoke is more dangerous than smoking, did you know that?'

'I'm a doctor; of course I know that. That's why I smoke. It's safer.'

Graham smiled. Fukuda rolled his eyes.

Kierzek drew hard and exhaled another blue-gray lungful of smoke with a sigh of satisfaction. If he was smoking two or more of those a day down to stubs the size of the one he'd arrived with, Graham thought, and inhaling to boot, it was no wonder he was wheezing. In fact it was a wonder he was still breathing.

'Now then, what else?' Kierzek mused aloud. Another

thoughtful drag. 'He hasn't been there long; less than two hours for sure, maybe not even one. There's barely any corneal cloudiness, no sign of a corneal film, let alone any sign of rigor.'

'He was seen alive half an hour before we found him,' Graham said, remembering what he'd heard from Lee.

Kierzek nodded. 'There you are, then.'

'Has he been moved, could you tell?' Fukuda asked. 'Or did he buy it right there?'

'Well, that I'm not in a position to say, I'm afraid. Could be either one. The body's too fresh to show any lividity, so, unfortunately, no clues from that. Maybe your blood-spatter people and such can help you there. Let's see, anything else? Well, nothing, really. I didn't see any other signs of injury than the head wound, but I won't say that for sure until after we've opened him up. Any questions?'

'Okay,' said Fukuda. 'Cause of death is blunt trauma to the skull. What about manner? Any ideas?'

'Hmm.' Kierzek's eyebrows lifted and formed themselves into inverted Vs. 'I'm guessing . . . homicide?'

More smiling from Graham, more eye-rolling from Fukuda. 'You know what I mean – any idea of the weapon?'

Kierzek shook his head. 'Not at this point.'

He seems like a good pathologist, Graham thought, *unwilling to commit himself to more than he knows.* 'Think it could be a pool cue?' he asked.

'Could be. If your people find a cue with blood and brains on it, better save it – it just might be a clue. I didn't see any such, however. Did you?'

Fukuda shook his head. 'No. And they were all racked. I didn't think to check if any were missing.'

'There was some blood, and I think a bit of matted hair on the rim of the pool table near him,' Graham said. He'd contributed little so far, deferring to the men whose turf and job this was. 'Could he have smashed his head – or could *someone* have smashed his head – on that?'

'Could very well be,' Kierzek agreed. 'Or he could have

just brushed it on the way down.' He sat there, wheezing and smoking contentedly, smiling at the others. 'Any more questions?'

'Not for you, Doc,' Fukuda said. 'Graham, who found the body?'

Graham looked at the notes he'd made after his hurried talk with Lee. 'A woman named Lynn Palakahela.'

The jaws stopped working for a moment. 'Lynn Palakahela, the golfer?'

Graham shrugged. 'Don't know.' How many Lynn Palakahelas could there be? he wondered.

'What was she doing in the pool room?'

'I have no idea. Not playing pool; there were no balls on the table.'

'What about Wyndham? Was he a pool player?'

'Beats me. Look, Milt, I don't know any of these people. I got here about an hour before you did. I only got to Hawaii a couple of hours ago.'

'Right.' Fukuda pushed back his chair and stood up. 'Well, something tells me we've gotten all we're going to get out of this horse doctor tonight. Want to come on down with me while we get the interviews going? Maybe I can find something for you to do.'

'I sure would.' Graham got up too. 'Nice meeting you, Doctor.'

'See you, Sam,' said Fukuda.

Kierzek gave them a pope-like wave of benediction. 'Go in peace,' he said tranquilly. Clearly he intended to finish his cigar in the clubby comfort and solitude of the card room.

'Bummer,' said Peg.

Lee nodded. 'I'll say. Kind of puts a crimp in the celebrations, doesn't it?'

'Just a little.' Peg uncrossed her ankles, took her sturdy, stockinged feet off the chair they were propped on, and reached for the cardboard pastry box in the center of the table. 'Want to split this last cream puff? I think it might be mocha.'

Lee shook her head. 'It's all yours. Two were plenty.'

'Not for me,' Peg grumped. 'I'm starving. You'd think whoever killed him could at least have waited till after they'd served dinner.' Peg hauled the sweet in, resettled herself in the chair, re-propped her feet, and went back to munching and musing, with an occasional sip of coffee.

They were in the barrel-vaulted main dining room of the club, all alone in the big, handsome room with its floor-to-ceiling gold-veined mirrors. At first they had been herded into the ballroom along with everyone else, but once Graham had vouched for them and had assured Sergeant Fukuda that they had no connection to Wyndham or anyone else in the Royal Mauna Kea, they were allowed to leave the ballroom (but not the building), once they had answered a few brief questions from the Hawaiian detectives. Graham had shepherded them into the dining room, had taken about thirty seconds to answer their questions about what he'd seen in the billiards room, and had hurried back to join Fukuda, although ten minutes later he'd returned with the pastries and two large Styrofoam cups of coffee.

'They've put coffee and sweets out in the ballroom for everyone. It was getting hard to hear because of all the stomachs rumbling. Anyway, I liberated a few of them for you. I was sure you could use the coffee, anyway.'

'Thanks, Graham,' Peg had said, 'but I don't suppose you could liberate something for us on your way past the bar, could you?'

But he was already gone, and since then they'd been alone in the big room, talking quietly, surrounded by the snowy linen and gleaming place settings of the perfectly laid-out tables.

'What do you think about that letter?' Peg said now. It had been several minutes since she'd spoken. 'Could that really have something to do with it?'

'You mean from those crazies, about the Mana Stone and Mother Pele and all?' The two of them had had a planning session with Wally in his office that afternoon, during which

66

he'd shown them the letter from the Hui Malu Makuahine Pele group.

'Yes. Wally was a little concerned about it.'

'Sure, but not from the standpoint of somebody actually getting *killed*. He just didn't like the idea of trouble-makers out there.' Her coffee, which she'd poured into one of the china cups on the table, was held on her lap, although she'd taken only one or two sips.

'But now somebody *has* been killed, and that somebody just happens to be the president of the club and the chairman of the board. Isn't that worth thinking about?'

Lee shrugged. 'I guess so, and I'm sure the police will look into it, but it just doesn't seem very credible to me. It doesn't make sense either. The club doesn't *have* the Mana Stone any more, right? So how were they supposed to return it? Besides, how would a member of this cult or whatever it is even get into the clubhouse on a night like this, without being noticed by everyone who—'

'Maybe he's a club member himself?' Peg interrupted.

'A club member *himself*? You don't really believe that, do you?'

'Wel-l-l . . . no, I guess not,' Peg said with a sigh. 'Anyway, why would he kill him here, in the middle of this Centennial thing, with the place crawling with people? Wouldn't he do it in some dark, lonely place with nobody around?'

'Probably, but, you know, when you think about it, that would be just as true for anybody else as well, wouldn't it? But somebody did it right there, right then.'

'That's so. The killer had to hope nobody walked in on them, and then he had to walk quietly out of the room. Did he have any blood on him? Was he disheveled? Out of breath? And he'd have had to pretend that nothing had happened. That'd be pretty hard to get away with.' She finished the first half of the pastry and started on the second. 'You know what that probably means.'

'That it wasn't planned? That it was spur of the moment, unpremeditated, a what-do-you-call-it?'

'A crime of passion, yes, although passion and Hamish Wyndham don't really go that well together, do they? You really ought to bring this up with Graham, Lee.'

Lee smiled. 'I have a hunch Graham and Fukuda will figure it out for themselves. If not, I'll be sure and mention it.'

'There's something else you might mention too, Lee, just in case they missed it. You know that very tall old man with that beautiful head of white hair? Very distinguished? Wearing a white dinner jacket?'

'Amory Aldrich?'

'I think so. Well, there were spots of blood on his sleeve. I noticed when we were all in the ballroom.'

'Peg, he was the first person to get to Hamish. He's a doctor; he was leaning all over him, trying to help him. Of course he'd get some blood on his sleeve.'

'Yes,' Peg said, 'but what if he ran up there to *be* the first person because he *already* had blood on his sleeve and this gave him a cover for it? It would also very conveniently explain why his fingerprints might be on the body, or one of his hairs, or whatever else those CSI types find. What do you think?'

'Sorry, not too much, really. He ran up there because I ran down to get him.'

'That doesn't disprove the idea. Being a doctor, he'd expect to be called.'

'Even so—'

'Well, you will at least mention the possibility to Graham, won't you?'

'I think I'll let you mention that one, if it's all the same to you.'

That seemed to bring them to a dead end. Lee, putting aside her now-cold coffee, followed Peg's example by kicking off her high-heeled shoes and putting her feet up on a neighboring chair. Used to wearing more practical footwear, she'd found her new open-toed, spike-heeled purchases a trial. She smiled wryly, thinking about her recent shopping splurge for the wedding trip. Since Graham had surely grown used to seeing her in golf-style polo shirts and chinos or shorts – and sometimes worse – she'd been determined to show him that she could look thoroughly elegant and feminine when she had a mind to. And that appreciative, almost dazed look on his face tonight when he'd first seen her in this shimmering silver and pale-green gown (the saleswoman had said it would set off her blonde hair and highlight the color of her eyes, and apparently she'd been right) had been worth it – well, almost. Elegance or no elegance, the next time she bought a pair of dress shoes, they wouldn't have spike heels. She gave a half laugh.

'What's funny?' Peg asked, surfacing from a reverie of her own.

'Nothing really. What a strange thing the mind is. I just realized I was thinking about my next pair of shoes while Hamish Wyndham is lying dead right above us.' Lee surprised herself by shivering.

'Oh, I doubt if he's still there,' Peg said in her best nononsense manner. 'I'm sure they've moved his body by now.' She finished off the last of the pastry and wiped her fingers on a linen napkin. 'You know, the idea of this being a crime of passion has got me thinking.' She leaned forward with something close to avidity. 'What did you think about Hamish's wife?'

'What about Hamish's wife?'

'Her age!'

'I didn't know Hamish had a wife, much less how old she is. Why would I know something like that?'

Peg shook her head sadly. 'Lee, sometimes I wonder about you.' One of the many differences between this unlikely pair was Peg's penchant for gossip and scandal, and Lee's total lack of interest. It wasn't that Lee disapproved exactly; she just plain didn't care. Too many other things came first. It was a point of view Peg had never been able to understand.

'Well, I'll point her out to you,' Peg said patiently. 'She's in the ballroom with the rest of them right now. Her name is Sally . . . shortish . . . a little dowdy . . . looks like she

might be part Hawaiian. Anyway, I bet you dollars to donuts
– hey, that's not much of a bet any more, is it? – that she
can't be more than forty-five.'

'Forty-five?' Lee's eyes widened. 'His daughter Grace has
to be older than that.'

'Yep. I'd put her at sixty or thereabouts. I bet she wasn't
too thrilled to have her father bring home a child bride at
his age.'

'You mean it just happened? He just got married?'

'This month.'

'You're kidding! Peg, you just got here yesterday! How
do you find out these things?'

Peg grinned back at her. 'It's a gift, a God-given talent,
totally inexplicable to those who don't have it. But what do
you think about my idea?'

'What idea?'

Peg sighed. 'That Grace killed him. You know, in a rage.'

Lee blinked. 'Um . . . well, it's possible, I guess. But the
same goes for her as anyone else. Wouldn't she pick a better
place than that to do it?'

'I don't know about that. Maybe he picked this particular
time to tell her he was cutting her out of his will, or maybe
. . .' She scowled. Lee could practically see a new thought
taking shape. 'Or maybe he picked this time to tell his *wife*
that the marriage was all a mistake – seeing his daughter
brought him to his senses – and he was going to have it
annulled, or dissolved, or whatever you do, so that now she's
going to be totally out in the cold after thinking all she had
to do was put up with the old geezer for a few short years
and she'd be in clover.'

Lee slowly shook her head. 'Peg, you're absolutely
amazing.'

'Ah, you like the idea. You think maybe it *was* Sally.'

'No, I don't,' Lee said with conviction. 'I'm just amazed
at how fast you can come up with suspects. Three in the last
five minutes. Two in the last thirty seconds.'

'I told you, it's a gift,' Peg said laughing. 'I don't know

how I do it myself. But you know . . .' She turned serious. '*Somebody* killed him, Lee. As unlikely and risky as we think it was, somebody did it.'

'Hello, girls,' Wally called from the doorway. 'They've grilled me and turned me loose. Can I join the party?'

Lee took her feet off the chair and instinctively pulled it out for him.

'Not necessary,' Wally said, rolling up to them. 'I've brought my own.' He pulled up, braked, and shook his hands out. 'Hoo boy, I've been using muscles I didn't know I had.' He looked from one of them to the other. 'I haven't interrupted anything, have I?'

'Oh, we were just figuring out who killed your club president, that's all,' Peg said amiably. 'We've got a few suspects for you.'

'*You* have a few suspects,' Lee told Peg.

'Are you kidding?' Wally said. 'A few suspects? There are suspects coming out the cops' ears. About all the new members since about 1965, to start with. Hamish personally tried to blackball about half of them, and the other half he made clear he wasn't that keen on. Besides which, if you'll permit me to speak ill of the dead, the truth is, he was a difficult, cantankerous old bastard, and there are very few people that he didn't tick off at one time or another. Come to think of it, I guess that makes me a suspect too.'

Peg and Wally both laughed, but Lee managed only a weak smile. Peg and Wally hadn't seen Hamish lying there on the floor in his own blood, with his neck twisted and his eyes half-open . . .

'The ritual,' she said abruptly, as a new thought hit her.

'The what?' Wally said.

'The ritual, your old initiation ritual.'

'What about it?'

'Well—' She reached for her cooling coffee and drank some down, unaware that she was doing it. 'Well, Peg and I were talking about it's being strange that someone would pick a time and place like this to kill him—'

71

'You're assuming it was premeditated,' Wally said.

'No, we've been all through that. Give me a chance to finish. Maybe there was another reason why he was killed right when and where he was. He was just about to explain the meaning behind the club initiation rites, wasn't he? The oath? The reason I was up there looking for him was that you sent me to find him to do just that. Well, maybe somebody didn't want it explained.'

'You're kidding, right?' Wally said. 'Whatever he was going to tell them was, like, a hundred years old, and nothing but this pseudo-mystical old crap anyway. Why would that get him murdered? Besides, he was the only one who still knew what it meant, so how could anybody be afraid of what he was going to say, if nobody else knew what it was?'

'No, I like the idea,' said Peg, ever ready to explore a new avenue of intrigue. 'Is that true, Wally? Nobody but Hamish knew the meaning of it?'

'As far as I know, yes. They stopped actually going through the steps of the ritual back in the thirties or forties or something like that, and he's the only one who goes back that far, so he's the only one who knows.'

'And he kept it to himself all these years, all these decades?'

'Yup.'

'But why would he do that if it didn't have any real meaning? Keeping a secret for that long is *hard*.'

'For you, maybe, not for a guy like Hamish,' Wally said, which made Lee laugh after all. It hadn't taken him long to draw an accurate bead on Peg.

'I'll ignore that,' Peg said. 'You know, I saw it in that big book in the library. "Whose is it?"' she quoted from memory. '"Yours and yours alone. Why must I seek it? Something something something brotherhood." How does the rest of it go, Wally?'

'You're asking me? I have no idea. I've never yet been to an initiation, knock on wood. As the pro, I try to steer clear of everything I can that isn't related to golf. I have a life, and I don't live it here. I suppose some other people know it by heart, though. I don't know. You could ask around. Of course, it's a big secret, so I don't know if they'd tell you.'

'I wonder,' Peg said, her eyes narrowing, 'if I could sneak upstairs to the library right now and have a peek at the book. I'd really like to—'

'Peg!' Lee said, shocked. 'You can't go upstairs. It's under police seal.'

'Oh, come on, I wouldn't go into the billiards room, I'd just—'

'It's probably guarded, and even if you got by, Graham would have your scalp, and what that sergeant would do to you I don't know.'

'She's right,' Wally said. 'I wouldn't mess with them.'

'They'll probably unseal the place tomorrow,' Lee said. 'I suppose we could get up there and have a look then.'

'That reminds me,' Wally said. 'It looks like you two are going to be off the hook tomorrow, and maybe the rest of the week. There's an emergency board meeting scheduled for tomorrow morning to figure out where we go from here, and given what's happened, I'm pretty sure they're going to want to cancel the rest of the festivities and probably close the club down for a few days out of respect. So you'll be on your own, free as birds.'

'That'd be wonderful!' Lee blurted. She was thinking of all the things she and Graham could do.

But Peg frowned. 'Now that's really rotten. Just when things were getting interesting.'

Ten

The velvety *slussshhh* of waves breaking gently on a beach late at night; the mingled smell of salt-laden sea air and fragrant blossoms; the soft, dry rustle of palm fronds high up in the swaying trees, a three-quarter moon low on the horizon . . .

Peace. Nature. And it was wonderful, a million miles and a thousand years away from nasty images of unpleasant old men gruesomely murdered in the refined and genteel halls of posh country clubs. Lee stretched, sighed, and laid a relaxed hand on Graham's arm. They were lying tranquilly, side by side, their backs against the pleasantly rough trunk of a fallen palm tree, in one of the small, sandy coves that lined the Pacific shore a few hundred yards from the Outrigger's grounds. Graham hadn't finished at the clubhouse until ten thirty – Lee and Peg had gotten away two hours earlier – but on the way back to the hotel he had stopped at the King's Village Shopping Center, found the Whaler's General Store still open, and had come knocking on Lee's door with a paper bag containing a baguette, a small dry salami, a package of pre-sliced Cheddar cheese, a box of chocolate mini donuts, and a bottle of Merlot.

His glimmer of a smile told her at once that it was Graham the human being again – Graham the man, not Graham the cop.

'I feel like a picnic,' he'd said. 'How about you?'

And so here they were at midnight, sated with good food and good wine. Graham had offered to fill her in on Fukuda's investigation during their walk to the cove – there wasn't much to tell, he'd said – but she'd asked him to hold off until tomorrow. All she wanted tonight was to be with him. And since then they'd been content to talk of other things, or not to talk at all, but just to be close to one another and let the calm and beauty of the Hawaiian night soak into their bones.

'Graham, look,' Lee said now. 'What do you think it is?'

She pointed toward the water, where a wavelet had spread, fan-like, over the fine sand. In receding it had left a leathery, gleaming object in the rivulets of its backflow. At first she'd thought it was a leather sofa cushion, but now she could see it wasn't.

'Hm?' Graham, who might well have been dozing, looked up to follow her pointing finger. 'I'm not sure. Maybe a . . .'

A larger wave followed, its surge lifting the object and sending it skittering on to dry sand.

'A sea turtle!' they both whispered at the same time. They watched the creature haul itself a few feet further up the beach and into a crevice in a rock outcrop that presumably provided it with a sense of security, then sink wearily to the sand, as if settling for the night. It was no more than fifteen feet from them.

'Did you hear that? It sighed,' said an enchanted Lee.

'Do turtles sigh? I don't think so.'

'Well, this one did. Anyway, isn't this wonderful? The moon on the ocean, wine and bread and cheese and salami, and you, me, and a turtle, all alone on a lovely Hawaiian beach.' She reached for his hand.

'Doesn't get much better than this,' he agreed, lifting her hand to gently press the back of it to his lips. 'You know what I'm thinking right now?'

'What?'

'I could really use a chocolate donut.'

She laughed. 'So could I, I guess.'

He opened the carton and they each took one. 'Too bad you didn't bring some milk,' Lee said after her first bite.

'Yeah. I had a feeling I forgot something.' He tossed a chunk toward the turtle. 'I say, old chap, won't you join us?' The turtle showed no interest.

'Graham . . .' Lee said after a minute. 'You aren't . . . well, you're not going to get involved with this murder thing, are you?' Then, quickly, she added, 'I mean, it's all right if you do, of course. I'm not trying to . . .'

'Absolutely not,' he said with conviction. 'I'm here to get married, not to work. I expect to lie around in the sun and be cosseted for the rest of the week. You're the one that's working.'

'Well, maybe not. Wally seems to think the club will call off the festivities – you know, out of respect for Hamish. That means Peg and I are off the hook.' She hunched her shoulders. 'I feel a little guilty about getting a free trip out of it and then not doing anything . . .'

'That's ridiculous. It's not your fault, is it?'

'Well, no.'

'And if they changed their minds, you'd go ahead and do what they brought you out here to do, wouldn't you? Whatever that is.'

'Well, sure.'

'Then knock off the guilt and enjoy yourself. Understand? You can't feel guilty about something that's not your doing.'

'Yes, sir,' she said, smiling. 'Oh, look, he's leaving.'

The turtle had emitted what sounded to Lee like another sigh, had laboriously turned himself around to face the sea, and was now lumbering and sliding slowly back into the dark, lapping water.

'Do you suppose I said something to offend him?' Graham asked.

'He sounded exasperated. I think he's annoyed with all this yammering on his nice, quiet beach.' She wiped her mouth with one of the paper napkins Graham had brought in the sack. 'I'm ready for another donut.'

He handed her the carton and took one for himself as well.

'Listen, if you're going to be free tomorrow, what do you say we sign up for a snorkeling trip? Give us a better look at those turtles.'

'That'd be wonderful!' she exclaimed, but then frowned. 'Oh, gosh, I hate to leave Peg alone all day, though.'

'Well, we could—'

'No, I want to be with you, just the two of us, it's just that—'

'Look, Lee, I know Peg. We'll invite her to come along, she'll be sensitive enough to come up with some reason why she can't, you and I will go snorkeling, and then we can all get together later for drinks and dinner.'

Lee stared at him. 'You're absolutely right. You're starting to know her better than I do.' She finished her mini donut and wiped her fingers. Without intending it to, her mind had started to turn toward the murder of Hamish Wyndham, and after a few moments' silence she said, 'Graham, is Lynn Palakahela a suspect?'

'Huh? Why would you ask that?'

'Because she was there in the room with him when I came up. She found the body. Isn't that the first person the police look at?'

'Well, you always do check on that person, sure, but—'

'Because I just wanted to say that I'm a hundred percent sure she didn't do it. I mean, she was really shook up. *Really* shook up. Nobody can act that well. She was practically in shock.'

Graham nodded. 'Which she'd certainly be if she'd just stumbled unexpectedly on to a dead body.'

'That's my point. So—'

'Which she'd *also* very likely be if she'd just bludgeoned said dead body to death herself.'

That hadn't occurred to Lee. 'But . . . if she'd done that, why would she have walked out of the room and told us she'd found him? Wouldn't she have stayed inside until she could get out without anyone noticing?'

'Lee, I was there when you talked to Milt Fukuda. You

told him she opened the door just as you were reaching for it. What makes you think she didn't hear you and Grace talking outside in the hallway and known she had no choice?'

'Well, I suppose that's true, but . . .'

'Lee,' he said a little wearily, 'I'm not saying she's under suspicion. No more than anyone else. I'm only saying it's a little early to rule anybody out.'

'Yes, I can see that. Let me ask you something else. Do you know about the oath?'

Graham looked puzzled. 'The oath? You mean that initiation gibberish? The old ritual? Yes, Wally was telling me about it when you went off to find Hamish. What about it?'

'Hamish was going to explain it, remember? That's why I was looking for him. Well, I was wondering if maybe . . . well, if maybe he'd been killed to keep him from revealing it.' Even as she said it she realized how absurd it sounded, and Graham's expression didn't help any.

'Let me guess,' he said drily. 'You've been talking to Peg about it, right? It sounds like a Peg sort of idea.'

'Well, yes, I have,' she said, a little defensively. 'But it was my idea first, or at least I think it was, and I don't see what's so terribly ridiculous about it. Is Sergeant Fukuda looking into it?'

'Sure, Milt's not about to close off any possible leads. He's going to see the board tomorrow morning, and he says that's one of the things on his list.'

'But he doesn't really think there's anything to it?'

'Well, let's just say I doubt if it's real high on his priority list. Sorry, honey, no offense, but frankly it wouldn't be that high on mine either, a hundred-year-old secret ritual or whatever it is.' He stretched, stifling a yawn. 'I thought you didn't want to talk about this stuff. It's not your problem anyway.'

'You're absolutely right, I don't,' she said, covering her own yawn. 'My only problem now is figuring out how to get up the energy to make it back to my room.'

My room. They were in separate rooms because Graham had insisted they do it that way until Sunday night, after the wedding, when they would move into the hotel's honeymoon suite. She still hadn't decided whether it was because he was such a romantic or because he was such a prude. There was a lot of both in him – not that she didn't find both aspects equally endearing.

'Sleepy?' he said.

'I can hardly keep my eyes open. I'm afraid the wine has gone to my head. I could curl up and sleep right here. Care to keep me company? Or you could always carry me.'

'Now that's a tempting offer,' he said.

'Which one, carrying me like a caveman with his woman, or going to sleep right here?'

He got gracefully to his feet and offered her his hand. 'Not carrying you,' he said, laughing. 'Not with all that salami inside you.'

'Before the meeting gets formally started, I would just like to say that I'll miss old Hamish, even if he did drive me nuts most of the time,' Bernie Gottschalk said. 'It's like the passing of an institution.'

From where Wally sat, still in his wheelchair, it didn't look as if Bernie was missing 'old Hamish' very much at all. At eight in the morning, especially after the long, stressful experience they'd all been through the night before, he looked even more coarse-featured, rumpled and bored than usual. The smelly, black, torpedo-shaped cigar stuck in his face didn't help either.

Nor did the felt-slippered feet, but since the board meeting was taking place around a glass-topped table on the terrace of his tackily palatial home in the Hulipo'e Estates, a couple of miles up the coast (the clubhouse was unavailable, being still under police seal), Wally supposed he was entitled to his choice of footwear. And mouthwear.

'Okay, people, let's get 'er going,' he said, using his tongue to roll the cigar from one side to the other. Bernie was always impatient to get started, always impatient to be done.

Wally cleared his throat. 'Well, let me say two things. First, Sergeant Fukuda has some questions he wants to ask you, and I told him nine o'clock. I figured we'd be done by then. I hope that's all right.'

An assortment of grunts and murmurs told him that it wasn't exactly all right, but inasmuch as they didn't really have any choice, they would have to go along with it.

'Second, there's a problem getting the board meeting started. I'm not sure exactly how you're supposed to proceed without a chairman.'

'I believe it's in the bylaws,' Amory Aldrich offered. 'In order to replace a board member who has, for whatever reason, not fulfilled his term, the general membership has to—'

'Oh, let's not stand on ceremony right now,' Lynn said. 'These are extraordinary circumstances. Amory, you're the senior member of the board now. Why don't you take over today?'

'Amory's the most senior member of the *club* now,' Bernie said, laughing. 'Unless you count the people with less than two oars in the water.'

'I'm glad to hear *you* think I'm still rowing with both oars,' Amory said glumly. 'I'm not always so sure. In any case, no, thank you, Lynn, I have no interest in presiding.'

He seems more depressed than any of the others, Wally thought. Well, he was ninety-one, only a year younger than Hamish. It must have been awful to have been called like that to the scene of the death of his old, old friend.

Or possibly the problem was that Bernie had failed to have coffee served, let alone pastries. Wally wasn't too happy about that either, and visions of good, black Kona coffee danced about in his head.

The others looked at each other. 'Not me,' Bernie said, holding both hands up, palms out, to ward off any potential outpouring of popular support. 'I vote for Evan.'

Evan looked up dully from his clasped hands. 'What? Oh . . . no, I don't think so.' His eyes went back to his hands. 'Sorry.'

Amory might be the most depressed of the group, Wally thought, *but Evan is the more profoundly shaken. Shattered.* He seemed smaller than he'd been yesterday – used up, hollowed out with grief.

'Oh, hell, I'll preside,' Lynn said, drawing an appreciative glance from Wally. 'The meeting is hereby called to order. Now, what do we have to talk about?'

'Well,' Wally said, 'I assume you'll want to cancel the rest of the Centennial celebration on account of what's happened . . .'

'Certainly,' Amory said. 'How can we hold a celebration with our president and board chairman not yet in his grave?'

Evan and Bernie soberly nodded their agreement. Lynn didn't look so sure.

'So you'll need to decide how to handle the cancellation costs,' Wally continued. 'You could—'

'Whoa, whoa, whoa, what costs?' Bernie had stopped doodling on the paper in front of him and looked sharply up.

Amory, in his slow, stately way, was equally rattled. 'I can't imagine we're obligated to pay anything, except for services already rendered. We've had a terrible tragedy. It's nothing we had any control over.'

Bernie took the cigar out of his mouth. 'Nah, nah, Wally's right. The reason doesn't matter. If you cancel you have to reimburse businesses who've already incurred costs, and maybe even reimburse them for lost opportunities. I mean, we had contracts, right? You don't just break a contract when you feel like it.'

'I'd hardly say it's because we "feel like it,"' Evan said, still speaking to his hands.

'Of course not,' said Lynn, 'but that doesn't mean we can welsh on our obligations. Bernie's right. He's certainly *legally* right.'

'Yes, I see that, but . . . well, you know.'

'I guess I see it a bit differently from the rest of you,' Lynn said smoothly. Wally didn't know she had it in her to be as diplomatic as she was being this morning.

At this point, one of Bernie's household staff, wearing an old-fashioned maid's uniform, complete with pointy little cap, trundled in the urn of coffee that Bernie had ordered after all, and the board busied itself pouring and sweetening gratefully, then sat back again amidst the clinking of cups and saucers. Only Evan, pale and self-absorbed, had taken nothing.

Lynn continued, turning her ballpoint end over end. 'Maybe we shouldn't be thinking in terms of how we feel about it, but in terms of what Hamish would have wanted.'

'What do you think we're doing?' asked Bernie, aggrieved. 'You don't think he'd want us to have a decent period of mourning?'

'Would he?' Lynn countered gently. 'Think about it for a minute. We all know how much the club meant to him; it's been the focus of his life for seventy years. Well, a Centennial celebration – I mean, a hundred years! – is a big event. You know how much he was looking forward to it.'

'Well, there is something to that,' Amory reluctantly agreed.

'And he most certainly wouldn't want to see us wasting money on services we never received,' Lynn went on.

Now you've hit the right note, baby, Wally thought, and indeed, Bernie beamed at her.

'Damn right. Hamish would be the first one to demand that we continue the party now that it's under way. That is, he would if he . . . I mean . . .' He faltered and busied himself relighting his cigar.

Amory, his brow furrowed, wasn't yet convinced. 'But what would people say? Wouldn't they think we were being disrespectful?'

Again, Lynn came to the rescue. 'What if we changed the name to *make* it respectful? The Hamish Wyndham Centennial Celebration. Something like that.'

Bernie thumped the table. 'First-rate idea. I second the motion.'

'We haven't exactly had a motion, Bernie,' Wally pointed out. 'Lynn, if you restated your idea as a motion, we could—'

'Oh, cut the crap, Wally,' Bernie said. 'What is this, the British Parliament? I'll vote for it too. What about you, Amory?'

'Me?' Amory said vaguely. 'Well, yes, I suppose it has my vote too.'

'Evan?'

Evan gave the ghost of a smile. 'I think Hamish would like that.'

'Great, that's settled.' Bernie whacked the table, setting cups and saucers to tinkling again.

'Wally,' Lynn said, 'that means you'd better make sure the women's club knows the horse race is on for this afternoon, in case they think we might be canceling.'

'Excellent idea,' said Amory. 'Very good. Does that do it?' He was preparing to rise.

'Wait, I got one more item of business,' Bernie said. 'Lynn has been great this morning. I move we make her acting chairman—'

'Chairperson,' said Lynn, but reasonably sweetly.

'—chairperson, chairlady, chairgirl, whatever you want, until we have time to call new elections. Did I say that okay, Wally?'

'Well . . .'

'Second,' said Amory.

Evan nodded absently and held up a forefinger to be counted.

'That settles it then,' Bernie said. 'Lynn, is that okay with you?'

'I'll be happy to take it on. I'll try to do my best,' Lynn said humbly.

After they'd left to take a break before Fukuda showed up, Wally sat for a minute on the empty terrace, slowly shaking his head. Lynn Palakahela as club president?

Whenever Hamish Wyndham finally did get to his grave, he was going to hit it spinning.

Eleven

Peg wrinkled her nose. 'Snorkeling? I don't know, sounds an awful lot like exercise. Besides, I can look at all the little fishies from here, and I don't even have to get wet to do it.' She gestured at the wriggling koi in the pond in front of them. 'Thanks, anyway. See you at dinner, maybe?'

'Absolutely,' Lee said, throwing Graham an appreciative glance. As usual, things had worked out just as he'd said they would. They'd made the offer, Peg had declined, and nobody was feeling unhappy or left out. She would have given Peg an appreciative glance too, but it didn't seem right to thank your best friend for removing herself from your company.

The three of them were having a late breakfast in the open-walled dining room of the hotel, overlooking a gorgeous panorama of ponds, streams, waterfalls and immaculately maintained tropical gardens that stretched down to the Pacific. Lee could see the cove where she and Graham had seen the turtle the previous night, and even the palm tree they'd leaned against. There was a man and a woman sitting on the palm trunk now, and two prancing little girls in the surf, which annoyed Lee, silly as it was. *Probably that awful Kimberly-Ashley family*, she thought malevolently.

'No, while the love birds are off playing, I shall bring my trusty laptop down to the pool and attend to my e-mail while sipping mai tais,' Peg said airily. 'One more unread message in my inbox and the thing's going to explode.' She looked down at her empty plate, then across at the buffet table, considering. 'Do I dare go back again? What do you think?'

'Why not?' Lee said, picking up her own empty plate. 'We're on vacation. I'm going back for more of those yummy fruits.' She smiled at Graham. 'Can I get you anything?'

'No thanks. That fourth piece of French toast may have done it for me.'

'The French toast, and the eggs, and the bacon,' Lee said.

'That too,' Graham concurred.

'And the papaya and the pineapple. And the muesli,' said Peg.

'True,' he said agreeably.

As Lee stood, a waiter came up beside her. 'Pardon me. You're Miss Ofsted?'

'Yes, I am.'

'There was a phone call for you. When you didn't answer, the gentleman who called asked if we'd find you. He left a message.' He presented her with a tray on which was a folded memo sheet. 'He said it was urgent. I hope it's nothing unpleasant.'

'Thank you,' Lee said, taking the memo. She opened it up. 'It's from Wally. He wants me to call him ASAP. Oh, boy.'

'Goodbye, snorkeling,' Graham murmured to the sky.

Peg reached into her pocket. 'Here, use my cell phone.'

Lee punched in the number. Wally answered on the first ring. She listened with only an occasional nod or comment. 'Oh . . . sure . . . no . . . no . . . really, Wally, it's fine. Yes, we just finished breakfast. See you in a few minutes.'

'I knew it,' Graham said with a sigh.

'Rats.' Lee snapped the cell phone shut. 'They didn't cancel the Centennial after all. I'm back on the job.'

'Me too?' asked Peg.

'Definitely! We're going to be running a "horse race" for the ladies' club this afternoon. I don't even know what that means.'

'I do,' said Peg. 'It's fun, you'll see.'

'I'm sorry about this, Graham,' Lee said.

'It's not a problem. We'll go snorkeling another time.'

'So I suppose you're going to call your new friend Fukuda and see if you can horn in after all?'

'Well,' he said, stretching, 'either that, or find some other girl to go snorkeling with.'

'Watch it, mister. You're liable to find yourself minus a fiancée.'

'Oh, in that case I certainly won't. Hell, it might take me *hours* to find a girlfriend as good as you, anyway. I guess I'll just have to give Fukuda that call.'

'Fun? *Fun*, you said? This is not fun, Peg. If this is what you call fun, what do you call torture?'

Peg grinned at her. 'It is a little chaotic, I grant you.'

'A *little*! This is complete and utter chaos. Except for the fact that they're using golf clubs to hit golf balls, it has zero resemblance to any kind of golf I'm familiar with.'

'That's because you learned to play on public courses. If you'd had a privileged country-club upbringing like these ladies—' she gestured toward the ragged chain of women slowly advancing up the first fairway ' – or like me, for that matter, you'd know all about horse races.'

'Well, I didn't. All I know about is golf, actual golf – to which this bears no resemblance.'

'Come on, Lee, lighten up, stop grumping. Look at them all – don't they look like they're having fun?'

Lee had to admit that they did, but once she started griping it was hard to stop. 'I'm glad *they* are,' she said, but then relaxed just a little. 'I guess I am too, in a way, now that you're here. Finally.'

There were thirty-three women entered in the competition, and the way it worked was that they all played at the same time. That is, all thirty-three women had to tee off before anyone could have her second shot. And then all thirty-three had to hit their second shot before anyone could have her third. From what Lee had gathered so far, the rule was that the first one to reach her ball was the first one to take the upcoming stroke, which was the one part of the game that made sense, inasmuch as it was difficult to bean a fellow-player if she was still behind you.

Difficult, but not impossible, and considering some of the swings she'd seen so far, it was only a question of time before someone got carted off on a stretcher. Besides that, the players weren't too fastidious about following even this simple rule, so there was a lot of thrashing and flailing going on at the same time, with golf balls whizzing every which way.

As if this wasn't bad enough, many additional members who hadn't joined the competition had come out to bet on their favorite players. They had turned into a highly disor-ganized gallery, both on foot and in golf carts, shouting out advice, cheers, and more-or-less friendly catcalls. (In Lee's kind of golf, a camera clicking at the wrong time, or a sneeze, or a too-loud yawn would bring a furious scowl from the golfer in question and a barrage of outraged *shushes* from others in the gallery.) This noisy traveling rooting section was supposedly following along on the cart path, but actu-ally they were all over the place, including in front of the golfers. They were either a lot braver than Lee, or a lot crazier.

In the midst of all this, Lee was supposed to be in charge. She was also supposed to be the referee, to whom disputes about golf-rule violations were directed for settlement. So far, thank goodness, no one had been very concerned with the rules of golf. And to make matters worse, Peg had been AWOL throughout the confusing betting and tee-off periods, which accounted in large part for Lee's uncharacteristic ill humor. Only a few seconds ago had Peg come trotting up the fairway to catch up with her.

'Where were you, anyway?' Lee asked now.

'Lee, sweetie, I'm really sorry I'm late,' Peg said, still puffing. 'I just plain forgot. I was trying to get a look at the logbook. I wanted to see that oath.'

Lee stared at her. 'Peg, the clubhouse is under police seal, you can't—'

'I know, I know, you already told me that. I wasn't *in* the clubhouse; I was trying to talk Wally into talking the cop at the door into bringing the book down to us, but no soap, darn it. He's as stuffy as you are.'

'Well, what did you want it for, anyway?'

'To see what it said, of course.'

'But why?'

'*Fore!*'

They both covered their heads and ducked as an errant golf ball whizzed by them, so close that Lee heard the *whish*. 'The green's thataway, lady!' a laughing male voice boomed from a streamlined cart with a snazzy burgundy racing stripe.

'Whoa, they should have given us hard hats,' Peg said as they straightened up. They looked prudently around to make sure there were no more golfers behind them, then began moving along with the slowly advancing line, keeping well to the rear.

'Why did you want to read it?' Lee asked again.

'Because it might have something to do with Hamish's murder, and I thought that if we put our heads together—'

'Peg, really, that's crazy. You're letting yourself get carried away.'

It was Peg's turn to stare at Lee. 'But you're the one who suggested it.'

Lee shrugged. 'That was last night. I was in a state of shock. We all were. My imagination got away with me, that's all.'

Peg's face fell. 'Well, I think you might have been on to something,' she said doggedly. 'It made sense. Maybe it had something to do with the murder, maybe it didn't. I'd just like to read it, that's all, and see if I can make something out of it. Wouldn't you?'

'Peg, this is not our affair. The police are looking into it. I spoke to Graham twenty minutes ago and he told me that Sergeant Fukuda talked to the board about it this morning, and nobody knew what it meant, because they were all initiated *after* they stopped going through the ritual, and if *they* don't know, I don't see how you can—'

'What had to do with the murder? Read what?'

Neither of them had noticed that Lynn Palakahela, clipboard in hand, had come up behind them. As a scratch golfer, one of Hawaii's best, she had not, of course, entered the horse race, but she'd volunteered to help out, and Wally had asked her to assist by keeping the scores.

'The oath,' Peg said without hesitation. 'The Ancient and Honourable Oath.'

Lynn's smooth, brown brow wrinkled. She tugged thoughtfully on her visor. 'Oh. You mean because somebody killed him just before he was about to "reveal all"?' The imaginary quotation marks she put around 'reveal all' made clear what she thought of the hypothesis, and of the oath.

Peg's defensiveness went up a notch. 'Well, yes, I certainly think it's worth looking at. Unfortunately, we don't have it to look at.'

'Oh, I can help you there,' Lynn said off-handedly. 'I have a copy. For what it's worth.'

Peg stopped walking. 'You do?'

'Sure. Everybody gets one before initiation. How else are we supposed to memorize all that hocus-pocus crap? I should still have mine.'

'Really? Could you—'

'Stop. Cease. Desist,' Lee said, putting her hands up like a traffic cop at a busy intersection. 'Can we talk about this later, please? I mean, this horse race thing isn't exactly my forte, and I'm having enough trouble just trying to figure out what's going on—'

A polite *beep* interrupted her, and the three of them jumped out of the way of two latecomers' carts that were trying to catch up with the action.

'—and I would *really* appreciate it if you two could help me out here, instead of doing the police's work for them?'

Once Peg got hold of something, it wasn't easy to get her attention, but the upward-spiraling squeak at the end of Lee's sentence did the trick.

'Yes, of course,' she said, laughing. 'There does seem to

be some sort of event going on out there, doesn't there? We can save this for drinks after. Lynn, care to join us?'

'Sure,' Lynn said, looking genuinely pleased. 'And I'll bring the oath along. Now let's go to work and assist this poor, harassed woman in the performance of her duties.'

The most welcome aspect of the horse-racing rules was that the wildest, poorest-scoring players were eliminated hole by hole, so that by the fourth hole, the field was whittled down to half its starting size, making it almost manageable and quite a bit safer. Peg kept her mind on the job at hand and she and Lynn worked smoothly as a team, keeping scores and providing Lee with moral support.

Once the beginners were out of the way, Lee found that the remaining women were actually well versed in the rules and etiquette of golf (hardly surprising with Wally as their pro), so she really didn't have anything to do but be there if questions arose. By the ninth, they were down to a single foursome, from which a plump, grandmotherly woman named Marge Merriam, dressed in startling chartreuse shorts and an alarming purple floral golf shirt, emerged as winner. The good-natured calls of 'Sandbagger!' made it clear that Marge had been a long shot in the race, and that winning wasn't something she was used to. When she stood up after retrieving her ball from the final hole she wore an ear-to-ear grin and her pink face was shiny with excitement. Lee, who had recovered her normal good humor by now, enjoyed clapping for her with the rest of the crowd.

'If anybody was actually dumb enough to bet on Margie, they're going to make a fortune,' Lynn said as the three of them trailed the rest towards the pro shop. She took off her visor and wiped the sweat from her forehead. 'Well, I'm sure ready for that drink, how about you?'

'Where do we go?' Lee asked. 'The clubhouse is still off limits.'

'The Lani Kai's right next door, on the other side of the eighth fairway. How about the poolside bar there? It's a two-minute drive. Let me turn in the scores to Wally – poor guy has to figure out the betting payouts – and I'll see you there in twenty minutes. I'll pick up my copy of the oath on the way.' She headed off, but turned back after a few steps. 'Order me a mai tai. They're famous for them.'

Like the Outrigger, the Lani Kai Hotel was another of the colossal, sprawling, lush, and gorgeous resorts that lined the Kohala Coast. Lee and Peg chose a table overlooking the azure-blue, three-tiered, terraced swimming pool, ringed by noble white columns and life-size statues that were (according to Peg) copies of works in the Emperor Hadrian's villa in Italy. They ordered mai tais for themselves as well as for Lynn, who came clambering easily up the stone steps on her well-muscled legs just as the drinks were being set down on the table with a basket of thick-cut Maui potato chips.

They clinked the fifteen-ounce glasses and downed their first sips. It was only Lee's second ever mai tai. She'd had the first one almost three years earlier, after finishing in the money for the very first time, and she'd forgotten how heavenly they were with their mixture of cheek-puckering tart and melting sweet.

'So,' Lynn said, looking at Peg, 'tell me: what's the connection between our sacred and revered oath and Hamish's murder?'

'What I said before: the fact that he was killed when he was on the verge of explaining its meaning to everyone.' She bit off a piece of potato chip and closed her eyes. 'My God, these things are sinful all by themselves. Who needs dip?'

Lee took a chip too and asked what she hoped sounded like an innocent question. 'Were you looking for him too, Lynn?'

'No, as a matter of fact I was bored. I figured there wouldn't be anybody in there and I went in to hit a few balls by myself – to pass the time, you know?' She shook her head. 'Boy, do I wish I hadn't. I'm going to be having nightmares for the next twenty years.' She took another sip; a longer one this time. 'Peg, look, if nobody else but Hamish knew what it meant, how could anybody be worried about what he was going to say?'

Lee nodded. 'That's exactly what Wally said.'

'You know, though,' Lynn said slowly, 'there is one person who might be able to tell you something about what it meant, but it's iffy. Philip Babbington.'

'Philip Babbington,' Peg repeated with a frown. 'I think Hamish mentioned him. . .'

'Why is it iffy?' asked Lee.

'Well, for one thing, it *is* supposed to be a secret. You have to swear you won't tell anyone what it means. Some people take that seriously. I don't know about Philip. For another, he's pretty ancient now. Philip's the oldest member; has been for years. He was initiated even before Hamish was.'

'I thought Hamish was the oldest member,' Lee said.

'Hamish was the oldest member who was still playing with a full deck. Philip's the oldest member, period. That's my point. His elevator doesn't necessarily stop on all the floors any more, but you never know. Depends on what kind of day he's having.'

'Do you think he'd talk to us?' asked Peg.

'*Us?*' Lee said. 'Don't drag me into this, Peg. There's a police investigation going on. I have no intention of getting in the way of it. This is *murder* we're talking about. Besides, I'm just not interested.'

'Oh, baloney,' Peg said with a dismissive wave of the speared cherry from her mai tai. 'This is not the sort of thing that detective's going to be interested in. Besides, you're every bit as interested as I am.'

Lee opened her mouth to protest, then closed it with a sigh. Peg was right on both counts, and Lee knew it. And she knew that Peg knew she knew it. 'Okay, all right, I'm interested,' she said, laughing. 'So, would he talk to us?' she asked Lynn.

'Like, now?' added the predictably eager Peg. 'When we're done here?'

'He'd love to talk to you. He loves to talk; you can hardly shut him up. What comes out, though, may just be a few peas short of a casserole; you can never be sure. He lives with his kid sister – aged eighty-six – in that cluster of town-houses that overlooks the tenth and thirteenth fairways. Their place is the closest one to the tenth green. Easiest way to get to it is to get a golf cart from Wally and cut across the tenth fairway between golfers. There's an access path from there into the community.

She reached down to her shoulder bag, pulled out a cell phone and a small address book, and dialed a number. 'Zeta? It's Lynn Palakahela. I have a couple of people here – Lee Ofsted, the golfer that's in for the Centennial, and her friend Peg—' Her eyebrows lifted.

'Fiske,' Peg supplied.

'—Fiske. They'd like to ask Philip a few questions about the Oath . . . Yes, I know, I've explained that, but they'd like to drop by anyway, and I knew Philip would enjoy it, so . . . Fine. Yes, I'll tell them how to get there. Say in twenty minutes?' She clicked the cell phone shut and put it away. 'You're on,' she told Lee and Peg. 'And now . . .' She pulled a rolled sheet of what might have been parchment, tied with a ribbon, out of her bag. 'Here it is: the great opus, for your reading pleasure.' She couldn't resist a disdainful shake of her head, but nevertheless undid the ribbon, unrolled the paper, and held it open on the table so Lee and Peg could read it. 'You can keep the thing, I don't need it.'

Both women leaned forward, even more interested and excited than Lynn had imagined. It was beautifully embossed in an elegant calligraphic script: a catechism, five questions, five answers.

The Ancient and Honourable Oath of Mauna Kea.
Whose is it?
    Yours and yours alone.
Why must I seek it?
    For the Continuance of the Brotherhood.

Where must I seek it?

> At the Beginning and the End, the End and the Beginning.

How shall I find it?

> First must you toward the heavens ascend, thence through Man's Ambrosial Shrine, to the Fount of All Wisdom and the Cavern of the Flames therein.

What must I do to earn it?

> To earn it you must unite great Telamon of the North with his Twin of the South.

If I succeed, what will be my reward?

> The Pride, the Honor, the Glory.

What must I swear?

> That none save the Brotherhood shall know the secret; neither friends nor family, neither men nor women, neither infants nor ancients. This must you swear.

'"The Beginning and the End, the End and the Beginning,"' Lee whispered as an unexpected shiver ran down her back. '"The Pride, the Honor, the Glory" ... It's all so ... so *solemn*.'

'It's all so *weird*,' Peg said.

'It's all so moronic,' Lynn added.

Twelve

'Yes, do come in,' said the bird-like, blue-haired lady, holding the door open for them. 'Philip will be so glad for the company. I'll take you to him. He's out on the lanai. His hearing's not what it was, so you'll have to speak up.'

A former grade-school teacher, Lee thought. She had that sing-song voice; that forced, merry trill that comes from too many hours in the company of six-year-olds.

She led them from the terrazzo-tiled entrance foyer into a living room straight out of an English country home: hunter-green walls, hardwood floors with lovely oriental carpets, hunting and golfing prints, and overstuffed Victorian armchairs and sofa. A sliding-glass door led to a covered outdoor patio with wicker furniture, where a deeply tanned old man sat in a wheelchair that had been made from a simple wooden kitchen chair – Lee remembered seeing one much like it on a visit to Franklin Roosevelt's Hyde Park estate. He was deeply absorbed in watching a lone golfer coming up to the tenth green. Two of the wicker lawn chairs had been pulled up near him.

Zeta Babbington stopped them at the door with a touch to Peg's arm. 'Now, I haven't told him about the dreadful affair with poor Hamish yet, and I'm not at all sure that I will. Really, what's the point? So I'd appreciate it if . . .'

'We won't say a word,' Lee said.

'Thank you.' She slid open the door and led them out. 'Philip, dear,' she sang, raising her voice half an octave or so, 'here's the company I told you about.'

Without turning from the golfer, he waved them into the two chairs beside him. 'Now look at this fellow, will you? Seen him before. The man refuses to learn.'

'Philip, dear, *sshh*,' Zeta said. 'He may be able to hear you. You wouldn't want—'

'Ought to chip to the fat part of the green, wouldn't you say?' Babbington plowed loudly on, undeterred. 'A simple bump and run on to the fringe, with a five- or six-iron, then two putt to the hole, am I right?'

You're right, thought Lee. Whatever floors the elevator might be missing, he still knew his golf.

'But will he do that? No, he won't do that. He'll use a wedge, try to loft it up and on, and he'll wind up smack in the right bunker. Now you watch.'

Into the right bunker it went.

'Damn,' the man said, loud and clear.

'Ha,' Babbington said with satisfaction as he smacked his thigh, and finally turned his chair toward them. 'Now, what can I do for you ladies?'

'I'll leave you all now,' Zeta sang. 'Can I bring you something? Tea? Coffee?'

'No, thank you,' Lee and Peg said.

'Warren, would you like some warm milk?'

'No, I wouldn't like some warm milk; I'd like a double martini, straight up, with an olive.'

'He loves to joke,' Zeta told them.

'Who's joking?'

'Well, I'll leave you now,' Zeta trilled again and made her exit.

'So, Mr. Babbington . . .' Peg began.

'Just come from the mainland, have you?' Babbington asked, apparently in the way of making polite conversation.

'Yes, last weekend,' Lee said.

'Come over on the *Lurline*, did you? Have a good cruise?'

Lee and Peg looked at each other. They'd looked through some Hawaiian travel material before they'd left and they knew that the *Lurline* was the Matson Line's most famous passenger ship for trans-Pacific travel, famous for making regular runs to Honolulu. They also knew that its last visit to the islands had been way back in the fifties, at the end of the golden age of ocean liners.

'Thank you, we had a very pleasant trip,' Peg said diplomatically.

'Staying at the Royal Hawaiian, are you? I believe I prefer it to the Moana, all things considered. But it's a toss-up, really.'

Now he was back in the twenties, when the Royal Hawaiian and the Moana were the only hotels in Waikiki.

'Actually, we're at the Outrigger,' said Lee. 'Just down the road from here.'

'Outrigger, Outrigger,' Babbington said, frowning. 'Don't believe I'm familiar with that one. Must be new.'

'Yes, relatively,' Lee said, figuring that, for Mr Babbington, 1985 was relatively new.

'I'll have to check it out sometime. Well, well. So what can I do for you ladies?'

'Mr Babbington,' Peg said, pulling her chair closer. 'We're here today because we're hoping you can do us a big favor.'

Even before she was done, he was slowly shaking his head. 'No, no, I'll tell you right now, straight out, I just don't believe women should be members of this golf club. Or of any real golf club, if you want my opinion. I know it's not a popular opinion these days, but there it is. Nothing against you ladies, you understand. I'm sure you're very deserving people, but you won't get my vote. We can talk about it, if you like – always happy to discuss things rationally; one thing I don't have is a closed mind – but I can tell you right now, as long as I'm alive this will continue to be a men's club.'

'Well, actually—'

'You're more than welcome to play as guests,' he added. 'More than welcome, glad to have you. But membership? No, I'm sorry, I'm afraid my mind's made up.'

'Actually,' they both began together, and Lee let Peg

continue. 'Actually, it's the oath we were interested in. We were hoping you might tell us about it.'

'The oath? The Ancient and Honourable Oath?' He scowled at them. 'You want me to tell you about it?'

Lee winced. They were about to get thrown out on their ears. The oath was secret, didn't they know that? Who did they think they were, sticking their noses into secret club business? And a pair of females, no less.

'Well, um, yes,' Peg said, 'if you would.'

'No, I will certainly not tell you about it.'

That seemed to be that. Lee and Peg looked at each other. Time to go. 'Thank you anyway, Mr B—' Lee began.

'But I *will* give you a hint.'

Lee had been halfway out of her chair, but now she dropped back into it. 'A hint?'

'That's what I said, isn't it?' His old face had crumpled into a cunning, happy grin. He was having a good time.

They both waited, but he merely continued to peer cheerfully at them.

'And what *is* the hint, Mr Babbington?' Lee asked politely. 'If I may ask.' Going on what Lynn had told them, she was afraid he might forget before he got around to it.

'The library,' he said, obviously well pleased with himself. He folded his arms and awaited their reactions.

'The *library*?' Peg repeated. 'That's the hint?'

He nodded with vigor. 'That's the hint. And that's all you're going to get out of me, too, try though you might.' A movement out on the course caught his eye. 'Ah! Now just look at this one, will you? Used to know his name – well, I think I did – but it escapes me at the moment. Should have hung up his clubs years ago. What is he, a hundred and twenty yards from the pin? It's too far for him; he needs to lay up with a short iron then pitch it on, but is that what he'll do? No, not him. He'll pull out one of his, what do you call them, these combination clubs . . .'

'Hybrids,' Lee offered.

'Yes, hybrids, and he'll go for the green in one shot. But

he can't handle those combinations clubs, I can't think of the name . . .'

'Hybrids,' said Lee.

'That's it, hybrids. So he'll slice it and wind up way off there in the left rough, in all kinds of trouble. Now just watch and see if I'm not right.'

The three of them stopped speaking as the golfer swung and hopefully watched the initial flight of his ball, but hope turned to slumped-shouldered dejection as the laws of physics came into play and the ball continued to its predetermined destination.

'Ha!' Babbington shouted, slapping his thigh.

With Lee behind the wheel of the golf cart they'd borrowed from Wally, they drove in silence, taking the long way back – not straight across the tenth fairway, but through the verdant community of handsome townhouses with their blue-tiled roofs and their exteriors of ochre or pale yellow. Some, like the Babbington house, looked out on the Royal Mauna Kea course, while others had marvelous views of sea and shoreline.

'Would you like to live here?' Peg asked out of the blue.

'Ask me again after I win my first major,' Lee said.

'I wouldn't,' said Peg. 'I like visiting, but I wouldn't want to live here. Too lush. I'd get tired of it. I like New Mexico; I like the desert. What do you think?'

'I think you're crazy. Peg, what the heck did that mean – the library?'

'Could have meant anything,' Peg said, shaking her head.

'I mean, did he mean library as in the public library, or library as in the clubhouse library?

Peg shrugged. 'Lee, I'm not that sure he knew what he meant himself. But my guess is, he was talking about the clubhouse library, and that he was referring to that logbook they have in there. He probably thought we were asking about the *words* to the oath.'

'Oh,' Lee said. 'You're probably right.' And then after a

moment: 'But is it possible the meaning's in there too? In the logbook? After all, you didn't look through the whole book, did you?'

'No, but how much of a secret would it be if it was right there for anybody to see? I mean, the book just sits there, out in the open.'

'Oh,' Lee said again. 'You're right. I guess we didn't accomplish very much, did we?'

'That's an understatement.'

'You know what I think? I think we ought to forget it now. We did the best we could. Maybe we should just concentrate on the centennial. There's plenty to do: the beat-the-pro challenge tomorrow, and then the glow-ball tournament – I understand that'll be a really big one. And then, of course, there's that little matter of the wedding coming up. It'll all be work, but it'll be fun too. So why don't we let Graham and Sergeant Fukuda worry about the investigation?' Peg stared fixedly out at the passing scenery without answering, so Lee continued, 'Well, doesn't that make sense?

No response.

'Peg? What do you say?'

'I ain't sayin' nuttin',' Peg said out of the side of her mouth.

Thirteen

Arriving back at the clubhouse, they found the police presence much diminished. Although the investigators were still busy upstairs, the lower floor had been unsealed and reopened, and Wally was now happily resettled in his office, which was tucked into an inside corner of the pro shop.

'The cops told me they expect to have the whole clubhouse unsealed by tomorrow, which'll be nice,' he told them. 'For a lot of the older folks around here, this is their whole social life. Well, pull up a chair, you two. Everybody says you did a great job with the horse race. I really appreciate it.'

'Forget it, it was fun,' Peg said, obviously meaning it.

Lee smiled dutifully. 'It was really . . . interesting,' was the best she could manage.

'So,' he said. 'Notice anything different?' He spread his arms, hey-look-at-me style.

When Lee and Peg looked blank, he pointed to the crutches leaning within reach against the wall, and then, patting the arms of his desk chair, he said, 'Look, no wheels. I'm getting around on my own legs. Well, one of them.'

They both expressed pleasure at this, to which he responded with a thumbs up, but then his face darkened. 'I just can't get this thing with Hamish out of my mind. I mean, who could have . . . why would . . .?'

'I know the police spent a lot of time talking to you. Did they have anything to say about it?' Peg asked.

'Nah, you know cops. They ask, they don't tell. They've really been grilling me. I kept thinking that any minute they were going to read me my rights and put the cuffs on me. They took all the furniture out of the billiards room, by the way – everything. They unscrewed the rack from the wall; they even rolled up the damn carpet and hauled it off. Even the goddam pool table, the one right by where he was killed – they had to use a crane and take out a window to do it. Did you know they did that kind of thing?'

'They have to take them to the lab,' Lee said, thanks to her long association with Graham.

'Yeah, I guess,' Wally said meditatively. 'They think he was killed with a pool cue, you know.'

'No, I didn't know,' Lee said. The memory of Hamish's bloody head came back unbidden. Could that ghastly furrow in it have been from a pool cue? Yes, she thought, it very well might have been. She jerked her head to get rid of the horrible image. 'Did they tell you that?'

'Are you kidding? Of course not. But they kept asking about the sticks – how many there were, did I notice any missing, and so on. Other people too. It was obvious that's what they thought. But what I can't figure is, how did somebody manage to walk out of there with a pool cue under his jacket, and nobody noticed?'

Peg deepened her voice and joked: 'Secret passage, of course.'

'Yeah, right.' Then a wan, nostalgic smile creased his face. 'You know,' he said slowly, 'when I was first hired, I was given a tour of the place – by Hamish himself, now that I think about it – and the old boy told me his father had designed it with a secret passage that no one knew about any more. He had me going there for a while, too; I really believed him. I went around for a couple of days twisting knobs and pushing panels.'

'Did you find it?' Peg asked.

'Yeah, right,' Wally said again, then came out of his reverie. 'Oh, I almost forgot. Lee, what with this awful thing that happened last night, and all the digging and fooling around that's been going on, we're obviously overdue for some kind of security set-up around here. Lynn wants to have a board meeting to talk about it, so I set one up for the day after tomorrow, before the luau and the glow-ball tournament. Five o'clock. Do you think Graham would be willing to drop by to talk to us about it? You know, give us some idea of the kind of options we have, and so on? We're really in the dark here. Just informally, I mean, although I bet the board would be interested in bringing him on as a consultant if he wants to work with us. What do you think?'

'I'll tell him,' Lee said. 'I'm sure he'd be glad to help.'

'Great,' Wally said absently, his eyes straying to some blueprint-like plans on his desk – irrigation diagrams, Lee thought – and the two women stood up.

'We'll be on our way,' Lee said. They had made tentative plans to meet Graham for drinks and dinner at the Outrigger in half an hour, and they wanted a chance to change first. 'Don't work too hard, Wally; you're still not a hundred percent.'

'A hundred percent of what?' he said. 'When was I ever a hundred percent?'

On the way out to the parking lot, Peg got her keys out of her fanny pack and pressed the button, producing a little beep a few cars down one of the rows. 'Oh, there it is.'

They got into the Toyota Camry she'd rented and clicked on their seat belts. 'Peg,' Lee said, 'don't even think about it.'

Peg started up the car and looked at her, oozing wide-eyed innocence. 'Think about what?'

'About hunting for a secret passageway that doesn't exist.'

If anything, Peg's eyes grew even wider. 'Now what in the world would make you think I was going to do something like that?'

'Partly,' Lee said, 'because I saw your expression when he mentioned it—'

'Huh? What did I do?'

'—but mostly because I know you and I know the way your mind works. Anyway, if you remember, we said we'd leave the whole mess to the police.'

'I remember that *you* said we'd leave it to the police. I don't recall signing on.'

Lee sighed. 'Peg, the darn thing doesn't even exist. It was just a joke on Hamish's part.'

'Right. Hamish Wyndham, the famous jokester.' As they turned on to the curving driveway that led to the highway, the clubhouse loomed, castle-like, on their left. 'You have to admit, it does look like the kind of place that would have secret passages, doesn't it?' Peg said wistfully. 'I don't see what it would hurt if I had a look around myself. '

'Peg . . .'

'*After* the whole place is unsealed, of course,' she added hastily.

'That's not the point. The point is, why do you want to waste your time looking for something that doesn't exist, and even if it did exist, that probably has no connection to what happened anyway?'

'Lee, if it doesn't exist, then obviously I won't find it, so what's the problem?'

Lee couldn't quite work her way through that logic – or lack of it – and, anyway, Peg on a mission was unstoppable. Lee threw up her hands in defeat and changed the subject. 'What's this beat-the-pro event we're supposed to do tomorrow, or don't I want to know?'

'Oh, it's fun,' Peg said enthusiatically. 'You'll see.'

Fourteen

'Grazing,' his old lieutenant in the Oakland Homicide Bureau used to call it, and Graham thought that was a pretty good word for it. It was what a good cop did at, or rather around, a crime scene. Not the CSI stuff, the tiptoeing around with tweezers, and weird lamps, and magic powders – that was best left to the techs who knew how to do it – but the browsing, the skimming, the turning over of leaves that you did in the general area, not hunting for anything in particular, but keeping your mind open to anything that might come your way.

And this, Graham was very good at. With Fukuda's approval, he spent the first part of the afternoon after the murder doing his grazing on the downstairs floor of the club-house while the CSI people continued their meticulous investigations upstairs, where the billiards room was. Since the building was at that time still under police seal, he had the lower floor all to himself, and could wander at leisure through the various rooms. At one point, Fukuda, on his way back to his office, stopped by to see how he was doing, but Graham had nothing to report. Yet.

The last place Graham checked was the boardroom, a relatively small room at the back of the building, which was almost completely taken up by a conference table, chairs, and a folding table along one wall. Under the folding table were two wastepaper baskets. The first one held two Kleenex, a crumpled cardboard coffee cup, and a scrap of paper with doodled horses (or were they puppies?) on it. The second one contained two more coffee cups, a defunct ballpoint, and six sheets of paper. A cursory glance at the first one sent him to the nearest telephone.'

'Milt? I've got something you're going to want to see.'

'Follow your nose,' Fukuda had said when Graham had asked how to get to the West Hawaii Criminal Investigation Section, which doubled as the Kona police station, and now, arriving there, Graham understood.

Unlike his old haunt, the Carmel-by-the-Sea police department, which was in the center of the beautiful little village, Kona's headquarters were on a side road off the Queen Kaahumanu Highway, in the flat, relatively unlovely lowland country on the way to the airport. There, in an out-of-the-way multi-use center, were gathered many of the necessary but unlovely functions that modern civilization required: the garbage dump, the Humane Society holding pens, a surreal, impossibly huge pile of wrecked cars, a trailer and heavy-equipment repair yard, and two great, steaming piles of 'organic waste.' But at least the police building itself was attractive – a modern, white, one-story structure, clean and well maintained, and situated on its own little island of neat concrete walkways and decorative plantings.

Armed with a cup carrier containing two sixteen-ounce, still-steaming cardboard cups of good Kona coffee from the Outrigger's coffee bar (Fukuda had specifically requested that he bring along some decent coffee), Graham was directed to the detective's office, where he was enthusiastically welcomed.

'Hey, great!' Fukuda cried, eyes brightening at the sight of the coffee. He was still wearing his Mets cap but it was on backwards now. 'Thank you! Can you believe I'm working on the *Kona Coast*, for God's sake, and I can't get a decent cup of coffee anywhere inside of five miles? They actually expect us to drink whatever it is that comes out of the vending machine.' He took off the lid, inhaled with his eyes closed, and savored a long swallow. 'So, sit.' He waved Graham into the chair by his desk. One more dreamy swallow and he put the cup down, then twisted his cap around, bill to the front. His getting-down-to-business attire, Graham assumed.

'Okay, let's see it.'

Graham opened the legal-size manila envelope he'd brought with him and slid out on to the desk the sheets he'd found, now loosely wrapped in several layers of tissue paper. 'Got this tissue from Wally Crawford, in the pro shop,' he said, gingerly undoing the wrapping. 'I've been extra careful with the papers. I knew you'd want to dust them for prints.'

Fukuda nodded his approval, then leaned forward as Graham turned the stack of sheets toward him, handling them only by their edges, and even then using the tissue paper.

'"Pele has waited long enough,"' Fukuda read aloud. '"Her patience is at an end. The time is growing near. The Mana Stone *must* be returned to mighty Mauna Kea" blah blah blah.' He scanned the rest, sat back, and reached again for the coffee. 'Interesting,' he said. 'This is the original on top?'

'Right; five copies underneath. Wally made them for the board members.'

'And nobody hung on to them? They don't seem to have taken it too seriously.'

'Obviously not.' Graham uncovered his own coffee and drank. He'd already had four cups of Kona coffee during the day, and hardly needed another, but it had seemed unsociable, even servant-like, to bring Fukuda a cup without bringing one for himself. He'd cheated, however, by making his own a decaf.

'Do you? Take it seriously?' Fukuda asked.

'If you mean, do I think that death and devastation will rain down if the Mana Stone isn't returned to—'

'That's not what I mean,' Fukuda said drily.

'Okay, if you mean, do I think maybe somebody killed Wyndham over this? Sure. Maybe. But not likely. Do I think there might be some *connection* between this baloney and Wyndham's death? Yes, I think that's slightly more likely.'

'That's the way I see it too. This might be a cover, for example, an attempt to send us off on a wild goose chase.'

'Well, that I'd doubt, although it's possible. These letters have been coming for six months; that's an awful lot of advance planning to mislead us . . .' He felt himself flush. 'That is, *you* – especially on a murder that shows every sign of being unpremeditated.'

Fukuda politely made no mention of the slip. 'Well, yeah, that's so. But still, it's an indication of pretty serious hostility – I mean, that's an out-and-out threat there at the end – toward the club, of which Wyndham was president and chairman of the board.'

'Right. That's what I meant by a connection.'

'Okay,' Fukuda said. 'Thanks for coming up with this. This is good stuff. I'll put it on the four o'clock plane to Honolulu. Our lab people will get it before the day's out, and I'll fill you in on what turns up, if anything.'

The cap was rotated backwards again. Graham took it as a signal that the meeting was over, but he had his own agenda; he wasn't ready to leave yet. 'How about filling me in on what's turned up so far?'

Fukuda regarded him coolly. 'Like what?'

'Like have you gotten an autopsy report from Dr Kierzek?'

He was acutely aware that he was treading on another cop's territory, which rarely failed to get the treadee's back up. That was certainly the way he'd felt when he was one himself. Moreover, as he knew all too well, policemen by nature tended to play things close to the vest. All the same, he felt that he'd proven himself and earned Fukuda's confidence. At least for the coffee, if not for the letter.

After a moment's narrow-eyed consideration, Fukuda relaxed and appeared to come to the same conclusion.

'I don't have the report yet, no, but Kierzek called to tell me what's gonna be in it. It was a pool cue that did him in, all right. He's ninety-nine percent sure. I guess he matched a stick to the dent in Wyndham's head. But the question is, what happened to it? It wasn't any of the ones in the rack, we're positive about that. No blood traces at all, and blood traces are a lot harder to get out than most people— Well, of course, you know that.'

Graham nodded. 'So then, where did it come from?'

'From the rack, all right, only it wasn't there any more. See, the rack holds ten sticks, but there were only nine in it, and according to the people we talked to last night, they were all there a couple of hours before.'

'Well, there's your answer, then.'

'No,' Fukuda said, 'the question isn't where did it come *from*, the question is, where did it go *to*? How the hell did the killer get it out of the room without being seen? The damn thing is five feet long.'

'Sure, but if you unscrew the butt from the shaft, the longer piece would be thirty, thirty-five inches – short enough to stick down a pant leg.'

Fukuda shook his head. 'Not these babies. Made in Germany back in the twenties. They're one-piece jobs, made out of solid European rock maple.'

Graham thought for a second. 'Well, then, if it was broken in a couple of pieces . . .' More head-shaking from Fukuda. 'No?'

'Did you ever try to break a well-made, hard-maple cue stick?' Fukuda asked. 'I wouldn't want to do it over my knee.'

'Neither would I, but I'd be willing to try smashing it over the edge of a pool table.'

'Yeah, but . . .' He stopped. 'That dent in the rim . . .'

'Exactly. What would you say the odds were that that dent fits a pool cue too?'

'Pretty good, I'd say. Okay, if that's what he did, there'll be bits of the wood from the cue in there. Maybe even a little blood from it, if he broke it at the right point.' He laughed. 'I wanted to fly the whole table to the lab in Honolulu, you know? But the damn things weigh over a thousand pounds, did you know that? So they're flying a tech out here instead, with a bunch of equipment. It's cheaper.'

'What about suspects?' Graham asked. 'Anybody?'

'Oh, we're not there yet,' Fukuda said. 'I mean, there are plenty of people who held grudges against the old guy. Between us, I guess he was a cranky old bastard who didn't pass up too many chances to tick off other people, so we have a lot of motives to weed through.' He glanced at Graham over the top of his coffee. 'What? You look doubtful.'

Graham hesitated. The turf issue again: he didn't like telling Fukuda how to do his job. Still . . . 'Well, I tell you, Milt. I know that grudge killings do happen, but I also know that they don't happen very often. And when they do happen, they're usually over something catastrophic, like killing a blackmailer or maybe someone you think got away with killing your wife, for instance. But what'd Wyndham do that was so bad? Blackball a bunch of people?'

'So you're saying . . . '

'I'm saying – well, I don't like to tell you how to do—'

Fukuda waved him on. 'Come on, come on, I'm not that territorial, and you've had a lot more experience with homicides than I have. You're helping me a lot, Graham, and I appreciate it.'

'Okay, then, all I was going to say was that if I were looking for motives, I wouldn't be looking in the past, I'd be looking in the present. Or the future. I doubt that he was killed because of something that's over and done. More likely he was killed because of something he was going to do, or might do, or just did, wouldn't you say?'

Fukuda, having finished his coffee, leaned back in his chair. 'Actually, yes, I would.' He hunched his shoulders. 'Look, I guess I was kind of stringing you along back there, not wanting to say more than I had to, because, you know—'

Graham laughed. 'No apologies necessary. I was a cop too, remember.'

'You make it hard to forget. All right, the fact is, we do have a couple of credible motives we're pursuing. There's

111

the daughter and the new-mother-in-law angle, for one, but I'm not all that keen on that one. Killing your father over a new marriage . . .' He shrugged. 'I don't know. If the daughter was twenty, maybe, but she's pushing sixty. My detectives think it might be her, but she just isn't at the top of my list right now. The one I like better – now, I'm not saying this guy is a formal suspect, but so far—'

'Who is it?'

'Your girlfriend's not going to like this, buddy.'

That caught him by surprise. 'I don't see how . . . wait a minute, you're not saying it's Wally?'

'That's exactly what I'm saying. Wyndham was trying to get rid of him. He needed three votes from the board to not renew his contract when it expires in a couple of months. He had one other member on his side . . . um, Bunbury . . . so that gave him two, and he was lobbying the rest of them. All he needed was one more.'

'Whoa,' Graham murmured, thinking it over. 'But you know, from what I hear, Wally's good at what he does, and he comes across as a nice guy too, very personable. I can't picture him desperate to keep his job. Not *that* desperate. He'd surely be able to get another one.'

'Don't be so positive about all that. A, he's fifty-six years old. Jobs don't come so easy at that age. B, this thing wasn't premeditated, we both know that from looking at it. And we also know that people can lash out in ways that don't make any rational sense, if you push them at the wrong time, in the wrong place.'

'Well, yes, sure, but . . . Milt, the guy was in a wheel-chair, for Christ's sake. He was down on the ground floor only fifteen minutes or so before they found Hamish. I was talking to him myself.'

'The whole time? Right up until your girlfriend called you to come upstairs?'

'Well, no, but . . .'

'All right, then. They have an elevator there, don't they?'

'Yes, but . . .'

'But how could a guy in a wheelchair brain somebody with a pool cue, especially without any signs of a struggle? It'd be hard if the guy he was trying to brain was you. Easy, if it was Hamish Wyndham. The guy wasn't exactly Arnold Schwarzenegger.'

'That's all true, but . . .' Graham let the sentence die away. He didn't really have anything to follow the 'but,' and besides, he'd seen Fukuda sneak a glance at his wall clock. He gathered himself to go. 'Well, I know you have plenty to do, Milt. Thanks for leveling with me. I appreciate it.'

'No problem. And I appreciate your digging up this letter. If anything else strikes you as relevant, let me know, will you? But whatever, let's have some coffee or lunch or something in the next couple of days, okay? It's good to talk things out with you.'

'You bet,' Graham said, standing and reaching across the desk to shake hands. 'You know where to reach me. Give me a call when you want to get together.'

Well, he sure was right about one thing, Graham thought, walking out to his rental car. Lee wasn't going to like this latest development at all.

'What? Wally?' Lee cried, her voice rising to a squeak, while Peg quietly choked on a mouthful of pita bread and hummus. 'You've got to be kidding me!'

'I agree with you that it's a long shot,' Graham said reasonably, 'but Milt has to check all the bases, and right now, as he sees it, Wally's his best bet. As Milt pointed out, the guy's fifty-six. Not so easy to find a new job at that age. Hamish already had the fat guy, Bunbury, on his side. For all we know, he managed to get somebody else too. That would have been three votes, enough to get rid of him – if he didn't get rid of somebody first.'

'Even so, that doesn't put him in the desperate category. Look, he retired from the Air Force after more than twenty years. So did Cookie. They both have retirements, medical, and all sorts of other benefits. He works as a pro because he loves golf. If he wasn't working, he'd be playing it. This just brings in some extra spending money; he doesn't depend on it for a living. Even if all that wasn't true, Wally couldn't hit some ninety-two-year-old man over the head – I don't care what the circumstances are.' She jerked her head in frustration and looked out over the view. 'Wally,' she muttered again. 'That's the craziest thing I ever heard.'

They were at a table on the upstairs porch of the Cassandra Greek Restaurant in the busiest part of Kona, sitting in the open air, but shielded from the sun by the white-and-blue-striped awning. Graham, after leaving Fukuda, had called the two of them and suggested they drive down and meet him for dinner at this well-known dining spot with the charming outlook. Across the street to their right were the cruise-ship-tender pier and the lawns of the Kamehameha Hotel, seen through a veil of rustling palm fronds that brushed the balcony. Directly out front was the bustle of Ali'i Drive and the little beach at Kona Bay. To the south the coastline swung in a huge, dramatic curve, all the way to the long, gentle incline of Mauna Loa's green flank, twenty miles or more to the south. Lee, continuing to fume, saw none of it.

'I mean, really, Graham! I can't believe I'm hearing this.'

'Honey, come down off the ceiling, will you?' He reached over to squeeze her hand. 'I already said, I agree with you. I told him pretty much the same thing. Give him time and he'll come to the same conclusion and go find himself a few more likely suspects.'

'We could probably dig one or two up for him in the next couple of days ourselves,' Peg said. Lee rolled her eyes warningly. Understandably, Graham hated it when either of them played policeman. The eye-rolling was in vain, however. 'I already have a few places in mind to look,' Peg went blithely on.

With painstaking care, Graham laid his pita wedge down on his plate and stared at it. 'I . . . hope . . .' he said mildly, but with an unmissable edge of steel to his voice, 'that . . .you . . . are . . . joking.'

'Of course I am,' Peg said with an unconvincing guffaw. 'You know me.'

'Because, while all this may seem amusing to you, we're talking about murder here. A *killer*. This is not something you want to fool around with.'

Peg shrugged but gave no immediate retort. She didn't like being ordered about, but even the redoubtable Mrs Fiske couldn't stand up to Graham in his masterly cop mode.

'Peg,' Lee said, thinking it was a good time for a change of subject, 'why don't you go ahead and have that last piece of pita? I've had all I want.' The truth was, she'd only taken one from the steaming stack and hadn't even finished that. Graham's talk about Wally had done away with her appetite before she'd even gotten started.

'Oh, I couldn't, Lee. I know I've had more than my share. I'm sure that's yours.'

'No, I really—'

'I'll take it,' Graham said, laughing, and did. 'I hate arguments.'

Not for the first time, Lee marveled at his ability to turn from the man of granite back into a wholly approachable and easy-going human being in a flash, and, along with Peg, she laughed.

'Oh, by the way, Graham,' she said, 'Wally asked if you could talk to the board about their security problems Friday afternoon. He's set up a meeting at five o'clock, before the luau. They just want your advice on what they ought to be doing, but he thinks there might be a consulting job in it for you, if you're interested.'

'Sure, be happy to. Ah, doesn't that look great?' he said as the waitress set down a folding stand with their three dinner orders.

But even Lee's 'Catch of the Day' plate, with its fragrant, browned piece of grilled ono and Greek side salad, failed to get her appetite going. While Graham and Peg tucked into their food with vigor, Lee glumly pushed things around on her plate, only occasionally lifting her fork to her mouth.

Wally Crawford, the man who had taught her so much and had helped her out of so many jams, was in trouble. If there was anything she could do to repay that debt, she intended to do it.

Fifteen

Unfortunately, an eight o'clock starting time for the beat-the-pro tournament made it impossible for Lee to act directly on her intentions the next morning. Not so, however, for Peg, who had no role in this event. The two of them drove from the Outrigger to the Royal Mauna Kea in Peg's rented Toyota, and with Lee's blessing (now that Lee understood that Wally was in need of some friendly help), Peg headed for the clubhouse to do some surreptitious investigating while Lee was out on the course.

It wasn't her precious secret passage that Peg was after – Lee had pretty well convinced her, or believed she had, that that was so much Gothic fiddle-faddle. It was the oath that Peg was interested in; more specifically, Mr Babbington's hint as to its meaning ('the library') – and more specifically still, the massive Mauna Kea Golf and Country Club logbook that was *in* the library and was, in her opinion, more likely than anything else to yield the oath's secrets. Lee had been right about that, Peg had decided. Oh, the answers wouldn't be there in any obvious way, no, but she was betting they *were* in there, if one could only figure out where to find them and how to interpret them. And this she was determined to do, or at least to try to do, to the limits of her intelligence and endurance.

At first Lee had been hard to sell on the idea. Graham's caution at the Cassandra against meddling in affairs that were properly the province of the police hadn't been the first such admonition he'd issued to the two of them. Besides, whereas Peg was a natural-born snooper, Lee was not. She hated

117

sticking her nose into other people's affairs. She'd finally gone along with Peg's determination to look into the oath for two reasons. First, despite Graham's reservations, she still thought it possible that Hamish had been killed on account of it; certainly, it was more probable than the ludicrous idea that Wally had murdered the old man to keep his job, as Sergeant Fukuda seemed to believe. And second, from everything Graham had said so far, the old ritual was the last thing on Sergeant Fukuda's mind, so if they didn't look into it, who would?

As for Lee's own activities that morning, she already had her work cut out for her, and they involved serving as the pro that everybody would try to beat up on in the beat-the-pro tournament. During the drive, Peg had explained the general concept, which was that the entrants – all thirty-six of them – were trying to achieve a lower (better) score than the pro – Lee, in this case – on four criteria: best over-all score, best score on the back nine, best score on the front nine, and lowest number of putts. Those who outscored her (they could use their handicaps, of course) would get token prizes consisting of medals and small gifts. The entry fees of $100 – $36,000 in all – would go to an animal rescue fund in Hilo.

All that was easy enough to understand, but Lee had needed a few minutes with Wally after she arrived at the club to get herself clear on the details. This they'd been working on for the last ten minutes, as they sat out on the terrace overlooking the first tee, where clusters of men and women, including many of the relatively younger club members, were stretching, taking practice swings, and generally milling about, waiting for the start announcement.

'So, after I play the first two holes with one foursome, I just drop back and pick up the next foursome and ride along with them on holes three and four, and so on,' Lee said.

'And on,' Wally agreed. 'And on. And on. And on. And—'

'Oh, eighteen holes, it's not so bad. As long as it's not a

118

real tournament – for me, I mean – I don't mind talking with people. I don't have to worry about keeping my focus, and it's nice to be able to help them with their games if I can. But do I keep my own score, or what? And do I have to keep separate track of all my putts?'

'You don't have to worry about keeping score,' he told her. 'Every foursome will have a designated scorekeeper. They'll keep your score along with everybody else's while you're with them, and they'll keep track of the putts too. When they all turn in their score cards, I'll add up yours to find the scores they have to beat.'

'Understood. That'll make it easier.'

'And if you'd ride along with somebody in each group, rather than use a cart of your own, that'd probably be a good idea. A lot of people would love a chance to chat with you.'

And I, Lee thought, *would love a chance to chat with a lot of people*. 'Will do. Now, do you want me to pull my punches? Should I let some of them beat me?'

'Oho,' Wally said. 'When did the once charmingly modest Miss Ofsted get so sure of herself?'

Lee flushed. 'Well, I only meant—'

'No, no,' Wally said quickly. 'I shouldn't have said that, Lee. I was trying to make a joke out of something serious. It's a habit with me.' He dropped his eyes from hers. 'I don't think I've ever told you how terribly proud I am of you. I mean, what a long way you've come from that dinky little golf course at Hahn Air Base, up in the Hunsrück. Remember all those worm castings on the fairways? You could hardly see the grass. And now you're famous—'

'Well, I wouldn't exactly say—'

'—and you play in the WPGL and you're right up there with the best of them—'

'I *definitely* wouldn't say that. I'm currently number forty-three on the money list.'

'Oh, I see. You're only the forty-third best female golfer in the world. Damn, that's really awful; you have my sympathy. I just don't know how you can live with that.

Look, I know I didn't have very much to do with all you've accomplished – you had a tremendous natural talent that was just waiting to come out – but at least I *was* your first teacher—'

'And best,' Lee said sincerely.

She hadn't known Wally could blush, but he did. 'Oh, hell, enough of this, already!' he said gruffly. 'End of today's meeting of the mutual admiration society. Let's go to work.'

He grabbed the crutches leaning against the chair beside him, got them under his arms, and started to work his way to his feet, but halfway up he lost his balance and plopped back into his chair. 'Not as easy as you'd think,' he said, laughing at himself. 'You have to learn how to do it.'

She tried to laugh along with him, but couldn't quite manage it. Seeing Wally – strong, capable, super-reliable Master Sergeant Wally Crawford – unable to lift himself out of a chair was unnatural and deeply disturbing. And now, as she watched him struggle up again – this time he made it – she saw with a shock how drawn and tired his face was. A fist seemed to squeeze her heart. His eyes were sunken, with dark smudges under them that had nothing to do with the bruising around them, and how could she have failed to notice how much weight he'd lost, and how his trousers hung on him? Despite his customary confident, upbeat tone, it was clear that his injuries and the strain of the week's events were taking their toll. And he didn't even know the worst of it; that a clever detective sergeant down in Kona had him in his sights as a likely murderer.

You helped me when I needed it, she thought once again, *and now it's you who needs it, and I promise that I will find a way to help you.*

She would snoop. Starting right now.

Talk to people. Get them talking. That was the plan. And with Lynn Palakahela being a member of the first group to tee off, Lee offered to ride in her cart, an offer that was cordially accepted. Lee still found it hard to take Lynn seriously as a suspect, but she was a member of the board of directors – the acting chair in fact; she'd be privy to all sorts of information that other people didn't have.

What she didn't take into account was that Lynn, as the sometime Hawaiian amateur champion, approached golf more like a pro than like someone out for a day's fun. The pleasures of a cozy chat weren't high on her agenda. Lynn didn't often enter club tournaments. There wasn't much challenge in them for a scratch golfer. But a chance to pit herself against an honest-to-goodness tour pro had brought her out, and she was tense and uncommunicative – just as Lee was when she was playing seriously. So far, all attempts at conversation had been politely but firmly quashed.

They were on the fringe of the putting green of the first hole, a par five, having each taken two strokes to get there. The other two women, who had taken four and nine strokes respectively, were closer to the hole. It was Lee's turn. Forty feet from the cup, she studied the big green. A difficult putt, not easy to read. Under ordinary circumstances, she would have stroked the ball well to the right of the hole, so that it rode along the flank of a slight rise and curved in a wide arc back to the cup, or at least to the vicinity of the cup. She could easily see it in her mind. A second putt from two or three feet out and she'd be in in four – a birdie. The one place of which to keep clear was the area to the left, where the green slid away and down toward the far fringe. A ball hit that way with any velocity would be caught by the slope, pick up momentum, and roll all the way down the incline to the fringe some thirty feet *beyond* the hole. A par at best, and possibly a bogey.

She leaned over the ball, moved the putter back and forth in a gentle practice stroke, took her stance, looked once toward the hole, once down at the ball, once again toward the hole, and swung her usual rhythmic, beautifully paced, beautifully aimed stroke.

The ball, following the curve of the green, went precisely where it was directed: two feet left of the cup, where it hesitated briefly on the cusp of the slope, fell victim to the inexorable laws of gravity, and continued rolling. All the way to the far fringe.

'Oh, gosh, no! Rotten luck,' Lynn said, but Lee could see her excitement building. Good, that was the idea.

She shook her head ruefully. 'Boy, I never saw that coming. That's quite a slope.'

By the time they were done with the hole, Lynn held a two-stroke lead and was clearly more relaxed and sociable. They took their tee shots on the second hole and sat on a nearby bench, their drivers in their hands, to watch the others tee off.

'That's was a nasty green,' Lee said. 'This is a challenging course you have here. Is that why you joined?' It seemed like as good a place as any to start the snooping process.

'Not really, no,' Lynn answered. 'Truthfully, I didn't even want to join – too hoity-toity for my taste. But everybody thinks of it as the *crème de la crème* of the local clubs – it *is* a fantastic course here – and right after I won my second championship one of the reporters in the post-game tent asked me if I'd ever played it. Well, I was feeling my oats, and I told him that no, I'd never played it, and I probably never would play it, because they didn't like native Hawaiians on their lily-white grounds. It was against the rules.'

'Really?' Lee asked. 'It was actually in the bylaws?'

'No, I was just shooting my mouth off. Being dumb, you know? I don't think it was ever really in the bylaws, but even if not, it was still damn true that no *kanaka* had ever played the course, let alone been a member. Anyhow, I dropped it, but the newspapers picked it up and made a big thing out of it, and good old Hamish came out in public and said there never *would* be any *kanakas* in it, not that it had anything to do with discrimination, of course. It was like that flap at Augusta a few years ago, remember?'

'Over accepting women,' Lee said, nodding.

'Right, but the Royal Mauna Kea had been through that

one back in 1965. Even then, believe it or not, Hamish was the general manning the barricades.' She shook her head wonderingly. 'He was one consistent old fart, you have to say that for him.'

'I think my ball went out of bounds,' called one of the other women, the one who had taken nine strokes to reach the first green. 'What do I do, again?'

'One-stroke penalty, Verda,' Lee called back. 'And hit another. After which you'll be lying three.'

'Three!' cried Verda mournfully. 'Oh, dear.'

'I told you, didn't I?' the other woman said with unconcealed satisfaction.

'So what *did* make you join?' Lee asked Lynn.

'I'm not sure, to tell you the truth. Everybody loves to think that I did it as a political statement, and there is something to that . . . a lot to that . . . especially after Hamish blackballed me on the first try; that got my dander up. But down deep, between you and me, I joined basically because I'm a real-estate broker, and I need clients – the richer the better. The Royal Mauna Kea's the toniest club on the island – contacts coming out the kazoo – and I figured it'd be great for business. Which it has been. You know how these fancy private clubs are.' Lynn laughed. 'Real clubby.'

No, Lee didn't know, but she wasn't about to spend time filling Lynn in on her own background, which involved exactly zero experience as a member of any private club, clubby or otherwise. 'It must have been rough for you at first,' Lee said.

'As far as the Old Guard, yeah, but most people have been okay. At least it didn't cost them any money. They didn't have to redesign the whole clubhouse to carve out a Hawaiian's locker room, or a Hawaiian's card room, or a Hawaiian's john, the way they did when they started letting in women, so people got used to me pretty fast. And business is business. I run a hell of a good real-estate agency, and everybody knows it. I get a lot of work through the club.' She smiled. 'I'm doing some work for Evan right now, and Evan's got to be about the most maddening, reactionary old geezer left, now that Hamish is no longer with us, so I guess I'm about as accepted as I'll ever be.'

When they walked to the cart after everyone had teed off, Lynn plucked a tiny golf purse out of a recess in the dashboard and pulled out a card. 'In fact, if you ever think about getting a place here, give me a call. I'm sure I could get you a great deal.'

'Thanks.' Lee set the card on the dashboard. Lynn started up the cart and they rolled silently down the path. Lee had gotten Lynn talking, all right, but she couldn't see that anything useful had come of it so far, and there wasn't much time left. She cast about for something else and decided on a more direct tack.

'Lynn, who do you think murdered him? Do you have any ideas?'

Lynn's face took on a hooded look. 'Got to be somebody in the club.'

'Yes, that's what the police think too.' Oops. She was getting franker with Lynn than she probably should be.

Lynn looked keenly at her. 'How do you know what – Oh, that's right, your boyfriend – your fiancé – is an ex-cop. I saw him talking to Sergeant Fukuda. He's helping him, isn't he? So, do they suspect me?'

It was asked lightly, but questions like that are never entirely in fun.

'Why would they suspect you?'

Verda sent her ball skidding another forty yards in something like the direction of the green. Lynn set the cart in motion again. 'I don't know. Hamish and I have never exactly gotten along.'

'If disliking Hamish was enough, everybody in the club would be a suspect, from what I hear.'

Lynn laughed. 'You have a point there.' She was quiet for a few minutes as they pulled up once more, this time to let both of the other women hit. But when they had, and it was time to move on, she sat, seemingly buried in thought.

'Of course,' she said softly, 'some people disliked him a lot more than others.' She started the cart forward again.

Lee's antennae quivered. 'Like who? I mean, whom?'

Lynn turned soberly toward her. 'Look, I don't like to make any accusations, and I don't mean to get anybody in trouble, but . . . if your boyfriend hasn't taken a good look at Grace McCulloch, maybe it's something he should do.'

'Grace McCulloch,' Lee repeated, frowning. 'I know the name, but . . .'

'Hamish's daughter.'

'Oh, yes, Hamish's daughter.' Grace was Peg's prime suspect too.

'You know, she was absolutely enraged at him. I saw her . . .' Lynn gave her head a shake. 'Oh, heck, I've yapped enough, Lee. You can ask her yourself, if you want to. She's in the next foursome.'

'In the next foursome?' Lee echoed. 'She's playing golf the day after her father's murder? Before he's even been buried?'

'Our turn,' Lynn said, pulling up. Their balls were in the center of the fairway, only a couple of yards apart. 'I think I'll go for a seven wood.'

Sixteen

Peg straightened up, did her best to knead the kinks out of her neck, took her coffee mug (with its third refill from the reopened upstairs bar across the corridor), and went to sit down at one of the two big tables in the library.

She had spent almost three hours on her feet, hunched over the massive logbook, unable to carry it to one of the tables for easier perusal because it was bolted to its stand, right through its snazzy, especially made in Spain, genuine horse's-behind cover. And she had found nothing. There was all – well, almost all – you'd want to know about the Royal Mauna Kea: the original mortgage on the property; the ornately embossed deed that was delivered when the mortgage was paid off; at least a hundred yellowing newspaper clippings about the club, going back to the 1930s (she had skimmed every one); a handwritten register of every new member's initiation from Day One: February 8, 1905 (it was interesting to see how handwriting had evolved, getting squatter, and less flowery, and more readable, at least to modern eyes); club championship records (even the indoor putting championship record); notations of members' deaths or resignations (a slew of resignations during the Depression, and then again with the tech bust in the 1990s); and just about every other kind of club-related document that could be imagined – including, of course, the venerable, original Ancient and Honourable Oath itself, a much larger version of the one she'd gotten from Lynn, exact in every respect except for the inclusion of a line at the bottom: 'Commenced this first day of October, 1908.'

Everything, in other words, but a key to the oath's meaning. As Babbington had rightly pointed out, it wouldn't have been much of a secret if it had been right there in the tome for anybody to see, but she had held hopes that it might be in there all the same, only disguised or coded in some way. But if it was, it was beyond her ability to decipher. She rubbed her eyes, teary and strained from trying to make out page on page of faded brown writing from the early years.

She sat looking glumly about her. Was she now supposed to go through every book on the shelves? There were probably ten thousand. Next to the logbook stand was an old-fashioned, multi-drawered card catalogue which would be easier to flip through, but what would she be looking for? She doubted very much that the one holding the secrets of the oath would advertise itself in its title. For about the twentieth time she unrolled the parchment that Lynn had given them, weighting its corners down with books so that it didn't spring back into its curl. She knew it by heart by now, but she kept opening it anyway, hoping that something would jump out at her. Damn it, how hard could it be? Until the 1940s every new member had to figure it out for himself, and if the members back then were no smarter than the current members she'd met so far, they weren't stupid, no, but they weren't exactly a gang of brain surgeons either. So how did *they* decipher it?

"'Yours and Ours,'" she muttered accusingly, staring at the words. "'Ours and Yours . . . the Beginning and the End, the End and the Beginning.' What a cartload of claptrap. "First toward the heavens go, thence . . .'" Her jaw dropped. *My God!*

She'd thought she'd been getting nowhere at all, but her mind must have been worming its way toward the light without her knowing, because it suddenly hit her: What if Babbington's clue wasn't *in* the library? What if the clue *was* the library? She banged herself on the forehead. *'Damn!'*

She hadn't realized she'd exclaimed aloud, but apparently she had, because the only other person in the library – an elderly, wizened gentleman in a dark suit and the kind of skinny tie that hadn't been seen on the mainland since the 1950s – swiveled his head toward her with a disgusted grimace and a recriminatory cluck. She could barely see him over the stacks of books in front of him.

'Madam! This is a library. In a library, I believe silence is customary.'

Obviously, the old guy hadn't been in a public library in a while. All the same, he had a right to read in peace. 'Sorry, sorry,' she said hurriedly. 'I beg your pardon.' She picked up her copy of the oath and dashed from the room and into the upstairs bar. Certainly she could get away with talking to herself there if it happened again.

'I'll have to put on a fresh pot,' the bartender, a cheerful young Hawaiian with a non-stop smile, said on seeing her. 'You cleaned me out.'

'No, I don't want any more coffee, thanks.' And then, although it wasn't the time of day she usually drank, nor the kind of drink she usually had, she ordered a cognac because it seemed like the right thing to sip while she put her thoughts in order. They didn't take cash or credit cards at the club, but Wally had given the two women charge cards. Then she found the darkest, quietest corner of the koa-wood-paneled bar, away from the two tables that were occupied, and sat down to think things through.

The oath, and everything in the oath, referred to the clubhouse; that was the key. She should have realized that when she'd heard that Hamish had been going to 'walk everybody through' the ritual right here, right in the clubhouse, just before he'd been killed. How could he 'walk them through it' unless the keys to it were all right there? Once you understood that – and how could she and Lee have failed to understand it? – then everything fell into place.

Where must I seek it? At the Beginning and the End, the End and the Beginning. Well, that was just so much gobbledygook for the clubhouse itself. Like most golf clubhouses, it overlooked the first tee box (the Beginning) on one side, and the eighteenth green (the End) on the other. The Beginning and the End. It didn't exactly jump out at you if you read it cold, but if you were aware from the start, as the new members would have been, that the event was going to take place inside the clubhouse, it wouldn't have taken much to figure it out.

From there, everything followed, easily and logically. *How shall I find it? First toward the heavens go* (in other words, upstairs), *Thence through Man's Ambrosial Shrine* (clearly a cutesy description of the upstairs bar in which she now sat) *to the Fount of Wisdom* (and what could that be but the library?) *and the Cavern of the Flames therein* – the fireplace *in* the library!

As to the business about great Telamon of the North and his twin of the South, that she didn't understand yet. She recalled from her long-ago reading of Greek mythology that Telamon had been one of Jason's Argonauts on the quest for the Golden Fleece. Was he the same person as Telamon of the North? And did he have a twin brother? Surely she could look it up on the Web, but really, none of that mattered. Her imagination, highly fertile to begin with, was now going full blast, stoked by the powerful, aromatic brandy. And she thought she finally had the answer.

If the fireplace in the library was like some of the other fireplaces around this mausoleum of a clubhouse, it would be an ornate marble affair, probably imported from some crumbling European chateau, and bristling with sculpted crests, and animal heads, and small-relief busts of mythological characters. And on it, she was willing to bet, there would be a head meant to represent Telamon of the North. And near it, his brother of the South. All she had to do was find them and slide them together to 'unite' them – she had seen similar things in dozens of old movies. And when she did, she had little doubt as to what would happen. There would be the sound of oiled, smoothly shifting stone, followed by the opening of a hidden door to – what else? – a secret passage, no doubt the very passage that Wally had failed to find and that Lee had scoffed at.

Practically trembling with eagerness to get back to the library, she made herself sit still and relish the moment. One didn't often have triumphs like this. She had persisted and she had succeeded, in the face of ridicule. Well, not ridicule; Lee wasn't the kind of person who went in for ridicule. But she *had* scoffed. Where the passage might lead, and what there might be at the end of it that was so important— 'The Pride, the Honor, the Glory' – she didn't know, but she thought she could make a pretty good guess.

And in about two minutes she'd know if she was right.

Finishing her cognac – it wasn't a bad drink at all, really, she decided – she set it on the table with a satisfying *thwack* and went with firm, enthusiastic strides out of the bar and back toward the library.

Lee had thought of Lynn Palakahela as very much the strong, silent type during that tense first hole, but Hamish's daughter Grace made Lynn look like the world's star chatterbox. She had said 'Fine', none too graciously, when Lynn had asked to ride with her for holes three and four, but after that there had been nothing. At least Lynn had replied to her comments, even if she hadn't gone anywhere with them. Grace didn't even answer, or if she did, it was with one-syllable mumbles halfway between grunts and words.

Until Lee hit accidentally on the magic word, at which the floodgates opened and the water, or in this case the vitriol, surged forth.

The word was 'father.'

'I'm very sorry about your father,' Lee said while she sat quietly in the cart with Grace near the fourth tee, waiting for Lynn's foursome – in particular, the hapless Verda – to get out of range. It was the last complete sentence she was able to get out.

'I hope the bastard's burning in hell right now,' Grace spat.

Lee was too startled and too shocked to say anything, but it didn't matter because Grace didn't give her the chance.

'Everybody thinks I'm heartless, an ungrateful child. Just look at the way they look at me,' (Lee hadn't noticed anyone looking at her), 'because I'm out here enjoying myself,' (Lee didn't think she was enjoying herself), 'with my poor father not yet cold in his grave. What was I supposed to do, turn into a hypocrite and go around crying and moaning about how much I missed dear old Dad?'

Without really thinking about it, Lee slid a little farther from her. Grace had an extraordinarily unpleasant way of speaking, making seemingly innocent words odious by screwing her thin lips into a sarcastic, poisonous little moue of distaste when she said them: '*enjoying myself*,' '*poor father*,' '*dear old Dad*.'

'That man ruined my whole life, did you know that? I've only just realized it. I mean, *really* realized it. All these years . . . I've missed Hawaii, my friends, the club . . . My grandfather was the architect, did you know that?'

'Actually—'

'If not for my wonderful, wise father, I would have married my college sweetheart.' Something like wistfulness passed over her face, but only briefly. 'And do you know why he wouldn't let us get married?'

'No, I—'

'Because Roy, my beautiful Roy, had a Hawaiian mother. Can you believe that? The bastard said he'd disown me if we got married.' A harsh laugh scraped its way between clenched jaws. 'And then – talk about hypocrites! – off he goes and marries his own repulsive Hawaiian sweetie, with my mother – and what a saint she was to put up with his tomfoolery all these years – dead only six months. Six months! Sixty years, they'd been married, and he can't wait to replace her with that, that . . . And the old goat's ninety-two years old, for crying out loud!' She stared through the windshield, at nothing. 'I mean he *was* ninety-two years old,' she said more softly.

This is why I hate snooping, Lee thought. *It's too personal; I don't want to know all these things that go on inside people.*

She was embarrassed at Grace's intimate confidences, venomous though they were, and thought that Grace must be embarrassed too, the way people tended to become when they realized they'd revealed too much about themselves to someone else. It helped ease things, she knew, if the other person then opened up about herself to even things out.

Which Lee then did; not about anything deeply significant (she was too private for that), but about some of her experiences on the tour and her apprenticeship under Wally. It quickly became clear, however, that Grace couldn't have cared less. She'd had her own say, she was finished talking, and she had no interest in the person she happened to be with.

That gave Lee the rest of her time with Grace to think, and by the time they parted company so Lee could hook up with the next foursome, two main thoughts occupied the front of her mind. First, Lynn was right: Grace had hated her father with a vengeance. If anybody had to be considered a strong suspect on the basis of motivation alone, Grace McCulloch led the race, leaving Wally in the dust.

There was something else, too. What had Grace really been doing in the upper corridor last night? Had she truly been looking for her father? Wasn't it possible that she had killed him only minutes before, and on leaving the billiards room had heard Lynn coming, upon which she had dashed into one of the nearby rooms – the ladies' lounge or one of the card rooms – to hide? And then when Lee had come upstairs and started opening doors, she had emerged from wherever she was and pretended to be hunting for Hamish herself, thereby A) avoiding being discovered cowering in an otherwise empty room; B) providing herself with an aura of innocent concern; and C) accounting for her presence up there, just in case anybody else had seen her.

She would most definitely tell Graham about this conversation, and he would certainly pass it on to Sergeant Fukuda. She felt no compunction about this. Grace had failed utterly to win her sympathy. (If she'd been so much in love with her beautiful Roy, why hadn't she just gone ahead and married him, and to heck with her inheritance?) If she had actually murdered her own father, she deserved what she got.

Unfortunately, however, the other thought at the front of Lee's mind pretty much made a hash of the first one. Unless Grace was simple-minded, which she didn't seem to be, it was highly unlikely that she was in fact guilty. What kind of lamebrain murderer would she have to be to go around publicly proclaiming her hatred of the man she'd killed only the night before?

Lee thanked Grace for the ride (no response), sighed, and moved on to the next foursome.

Peg strode back into the library with perhaps a little too much verve, thereby earning a malevolent glare from the frail old gent behind the books, which she saw now were, improbably enough, about mountain climbing and survival skills.

She smiled civilly at him and put a finger to her lips to indicate that she would be as quiet as a mouse this time. He made a doubtful huffing noise, after which his head disappeared behind a propped-open copy of *A Hiking and Climbing Guide to the Western Himalayas*. Closing her eyes, then drawing and letting out a breath to make the moment last longer, she turned to look at the fireplace.

'*Damn!*' she exclaimed.

The old head came up again, accompanied by a sigh. 'Madam, is there some problem?'

'Yes, there's a problem!' she howled. 'There *isn't* any fireplace in the library! How can that *be*?'

He now realized he was dealing with a lunatic. 'No, no, there doesn't seem to be, does there?' he said soothingly. 'There's one in the billiards room, however. Perhaps you could try there?'

Seventeen

The next person that Lee rode with, a freckled, frizzy-haired young banker – well, in his early forties; young for the Royal Mauna Kea – named Ralph (pronounced *Rafe*, la-de-da English style), who had been a member for less than a year, was a lot more affable than Grace had been. Like the others that followed him, he was eager to speculate on Hamish's murder and to ask *her* questions. (He and everyone else seemed to know about her relationship to Graham.) But as someone who barely knew Hamish, Ralph had little of value to contribute.

Except for one interesting detail: when Lee mentioned the oath, it came as a surprise to him that Hamish had been going to explain its meaning the previous night. He had no idea that had been on the agenda. Neither did the rest of his foursome. Nor the next foursome, nor the next, nor the next, nor the next. Nobody, it seemed, had known.

Well, that wasn't quite true. Wally had known, of course; that was why he had sent her looking for Hamish. And Lynn had known; over mai tais at the Lani Kai, she had referred ironically to Hamish's intention to 'reveal all.' So who else had known? Anyone? If Wally and Lynn (and Hamish, of course) had been in on it, did that suggest that the rest of the board had known too?

By simple dumb luck, the last group of the day, with whom she was to play the final two holes, was a threesome, comprised of the remaining members of the board: plump, affable Evan Bunbury and big-boned but frail Amory Aldrich, with both of whom she'd played a round of golf a couple of days earlier, and the stogie-puffing Bernie Gottschalk, whom she had met only briefly the night before, when she'd gone looking for Hamish.

Her plan had been to bring up the subject of the oath – casually, of course – early in play, but it didn't work out that way. Almost as soon as she joined them on the seventeenth hole, they asked her to tee off first. This was a common enough request when she played with amateurs. They liked to watch a grooved, professional swing before they came up themselves, probably in hopes that at least some of it might rub off. So up she stepped to the tee with her four-iron. The hole was a lovely one, a 190-yard par three, with the tee box on a palm-shaded hill overlooking a reed-filled pond, beyond which was a lush, pear-shaped green.

With her mind on just how she was going to phrase her questions about the oath, she distractedly lined up and took a half-hearted practice swing. The three men watched from the bench behind her.

'Look out for the wind, Lee,' Amory called. 'The trades can trip you up this time of year.'

'Hey, Amory, no hints!' Bernie complained. 'I got a big-time side bet going with Evan here that I can beat her. Counting my handicap, I mean,' he added.

'Oh, big time,' mocked Evan. 'A whole ten dollars.'

They were trying their best to be friendly and amusing, but it was apparent that they were harder hit by Hamish's death than were any of the other groups she'd played with. They were probably in the match simply because they felt it was their duty as board members to participate in what was, after all, part of a memorial tribute to Hamish, but they were obviously only going through the motions. Their hearts, it was clear, weren't in it.

'Thanks, Amory,' she said. 'I can use all the help I can get.'

She took an absent-minded waggle – *her* heart wasn't exactly in it either – and casually swung, at about three-quarter strength. If someone had asked her whether she were going directly for the green or was trying to land it short and run it up, she would have been a bit vague on the answer. All the same, it was a good swing, if rather too relaxed. There was the usual quiet *clook* of a well-struck golf ball, a sound she never tired of, and the brilliant white sphere arced prettily over the pond, came softly down on the green about fifteen feet from the hole, bounced once, bounced twice, rolled the last few feet, gently nudged against the pole of the flag, balanced on the rim of the hole for a moment, and vanished.

A hole in one.

After a stunned silence, they all spoke up at once.

'Damn it, Amory,' Bernie said, 'this is your fault. There goes my ten bucks.' He sighed. 'You know, I've been playing for thirty years, and I've never gotten one of those.'

'Try sixty,' said Amory, summoning up a laugh, 'like me.'

'I got one once,' Evan said wistfully. 'Right here on this very hole. I needed it, too. That was the year I won the club championship . . . by exactly one stroke.' He smiled at the distant memory. 'I was sixteen years old, the youngest champion ever, right up to this day. Wasn't even a member in my own right at the time – too young.' He shook his head. 'Talk about being excited. I thought I was on my way to being the next Bobby Jones.'

'Believe it or not,' Lee said, 'I'm pretty excited myself.' This was her third hole in one, but she didn't know if she was more pleased with sinking it, or more annoyed that she couldn't have saved it for when it counted. Holes in one were completely luck, as opposed to skill, which meant you were entitled to only so many of them in a lifetime, and she hated using up one of them in the Royal Mauna beat-the-pro tournament.

Evan was next up, and Lee joined the other two on the bench to watch. 'It was good to see Evan smile there,' Amory said. 'He's been in a funk all day. He and Hamish go back a long, long way.'

'Even longer than you did,' Bernie said. 'Since the Jurassic, at least. Oh, hey, hell of a shot, Evan.'

Evan, even if not the golfer he'd been at sixteen, was still something to see at eighty. He had swung delicately, but with beautiful timing and balance, and had put the ball on the green no more than three feet from the hole. A sure birdie. He came back looking moderately pleased with himself, but in a melancholy way. 'Once upon a time I could have done that with a four-iron too. Now it takes a three-wood, and I'm lucky I got there with that.'

'It was a beautiful shot, whatever you used,' Lee told him. 'It would have been beautiful with a broomstick.'

Amory went next and landed the ball on the fringe – a decent shot. That left only Bernie. Though not much more than half their age, he was a far less proficient golfer than Amory or Evan. He wielded his club like a man beating down a threatening giant earthworm. The violently assaulted ball popped out from under the club, bounded down the hill, and fell into the pond with a melancholy *ploop*.

'Maybe I *should* try a broomstick,' Bernie grumbled, coming back to the bench.

Evan offered Lee a lift in his cart, which she accepted. At first they chatted cursorily about golf, but on their ride to the eighteenth tee, he suddenly turned to her and blurted: 'You know what I can't understand? Why did he go to the damned billiards room in the first place?' Lee could see that he was close to tears. The tendons at the sides of his neck stuck out like ropes, even through the layers of fat. 'He didn't play billiards. What was he doing in there? He was sitting in the bar with us, he went to get his bifocals, and the next thing we knew . . . ah, what the hell.' He shook his head and fell silent.

Lee saw her chance to get the information she was after. 'Could it be because it had something to do with the oath?' She waited for his reaction.

Evan shook his head confusedly. 'I don't . . .'

'Well, he was going to explain the meaning of it, wasn't he? Maybe he was arranging something, or getting something ready, you know?'

Evan nodded, the well-fleshed head going slowly up and down once, twice, three times. 'Well, yes, that could be, I suppose.'

'So you *did* know he was going explain it?' Lee asked off-handedly.

'Yes, of course. He told us at the board meeting yesterday morning.' He fell silent again, mentally chewing this over, but as they pulled up to the tee box, he turned to her again with something like distrust on his face. 'Do you mind my asking how you knew he was going to do that? It was going to be a surprise, a secret. Only the people at the board meeting were supposed to know.'

'Oh, I—' She was about to say that she'd heard it from Wally before she remembered that Evan was the other board member who'd been ready to vote for terminating him. She switched gears, none too gracefully. 'I think I must have heard it from . . . oh, from Graham. I mean, afterwards, of course. Somebody must have . . . um . . . mentioned it to them . . . to the . . . um . . . police.'

'I see,' Evan said, obviously less than satisfied.

But Lee was satisfied. She'd had her question answered.

Only the people at the board meeting were supposed to know.

Eighteen

Graham was taking it easy. He'd had a solitary but leisurely lunch at the hotel, then spent twenty minutes in the sauna, and followed it up with a swim. Now, relaxed and loose muscled, clad in his damp swim trunks and a terrycloth robe from his room, he was on the shaded Outrigger terrace with his laptop and a lemonade, working up his security presentation to give to the board the next day, when his cell phone beeped on the table beside the laptop.

'Graham, this is Milt Fukuda. Listen, I only have a minute, but I wanted to fill you in on some of the lab results we got. I think you'll be interested.'

'I am.' Graham hit the Save button on the laptop and turned it off. He was pleased that Milt was calling him. He hadn't really expected that he would. 'What do you have?'

'Well, first of all, you were right on target about a couple of things. That was Hamish's blood on the rim of the table. It wasn't spatter, it was from contact. They say it doesn't look as if he hit it hard enough to kill him, but that his head was already busted and he probably brushed against it on the way down.'

Interesting, Graham thought, but it didn't give them anything useful.

'Which doesn't really give us anything useful,' Fukuda echoed out loud, 'but I thought you'd want to know. Now, remember that dent in the rim?'

'Sure. Narrow, about an inch long.'

'Right. Well, you were right about that, too. The table's made out of mahogany, but there are maple fibers driven into the wood of the dent. So they used one of the other sticks from the rack to see if they fitted into the dent—'

'The way Kierzek did with the dent in Wyndham's head.'

'Yeah, and they got the same results. The cue stick fitted. It's actually two dents, one inside the other and one slightly smaller in diameter than the other, so they think that—'

'He broke it in *three* pieces, which took two smashes, and of course one would be a little narrower than the other, since a cue stick tapers.'

'You got it.'

'Well, that's interesting, Milt. That would explain how he got it out of there. Hey, I very much appreciate your keeping me in the loop on this.'

'You think that's interesting?' Graham heard gum crack. 'Listen to this. The lab guys picked up some reddish dirt from the carpet, from right near where we found Wyndham, and it's all full of . . . uh . . . what does it say here? Titano . . . titanomaghemite, and sugar cane residue, and soil additives and such, the upshot of which is that they can tell exactly what part of the Big Island it came from, and that part is a little agricultural area up around Kapa'au, where they used to raise sugar cane, then went to coffee, then went to watermelon, and now it just grows eucalyptus.'

'Uh-huh. And where is Kapa'au?'

'Up in the boondocks, the very north tip of the island. It's a good thirty-five miles from the clubhouse. An hour's drive.'

'Okay, so what does that tell you?' Graham asked. 'Anybody could have been walking around up there and gotten it on their shoes, couldn't they?'

'Gimme a chance to finish, will you? The thing is, the dirt is *fresh*. It wasn't all ground into the carpet, and the cleaning guy swears on his life that it wasn't there at five o'clock when he went over the upstairs. And there's a lot of it; he would have noticed. That's the funny part. The lab says this didn't come off just one guy's shoes. They figure there had to be at least four. Guys, I mean, not shoes. And Wyndham's shoes – he was wearing those patent-leather ones – are clean.'

'I see,' Graham said. 'So you're telling me there were at least four people up there just about the time Wyndham was killed, and they'd all come pretty much straight from Kapa'au.'

'Maybe even five. It's weird. I've had my guys asking people what the connection to Kapa'au could be and all they drew was blanks. But . . .'

'But you've come up with one.'

'You better believe it. Kapa'au is holy territory to a lot of Hawaiians. It's the birthplace of King Kamehameha the Great.' Fukuda let that sink in before going on. 'And here's something else. Wyndham didn't have any of the dirt on his shoes, no, but it was all over his clothes. So how do you figure that? Did they *handle* him? Was this some kind of ritual execution? Is it related to that crazy Mana Stone thing after all?' Graham heard Fukuda's gum crack. 'So, give me your take on it.'

'All right, I think you're on to something here. That's all too bizarre to be a coincidence. But as to a ritual execution, I don't think so. Ritual executions are planned. They would have come with a weapon; they wouldn't have grabbed a pool cue off a rack.'

'That's probably true.'

'And one other problem: how did they get in and out without being spotted? These would be strangers, outsiders—'

'Well, now, that brings up the next thing,' Fukuda said happily. 'You know—'

'You're enjoying this, aren't you?' Graham said. 'You're having a good time.'

'Are you kidding? I *love* this stuff. Don't you?'

'I guess I do,' Graham admitted with a smile.

'So, as I was saying, you know that letter from the cult, about how Mama Pele's gonna get them? Well, the lab did some quick work on it. The paper that it's on is called . . . let me see . . .' Papers shuffled. 'It's called laid paper. You press the water out of it over a wire screen or something; I don't know all the details. It was real popular in the nineteenth century, and there's this outfit in Indonesia – no, in

Malaysia – that makes it exactly like they did then, by hand.'

'And that's what the letter was written on?'

'That's what the letter was on. *Very* expensive. There's this little embossed stationer's mark up in the left corner, and it's got the company's name on it. And this company, which sells mostly to Asia and Europe, has one outlet in all of Hawaii: Hibiscus Trading and Import in Honolulu. And Hibiscus Trading and Import has had only *two* orders for this fancy, special-order paper in the last ten years. One went to a vanity-press publisher, which used it to put out a special edition of an autobiography by a lady who'd taken two hundred and twenty-five luxury cruises—'

'I can't wait to read that one. I see you've been doing some quick work too, Milt.'

'Thank you. And the other went to – get ready for this – a certain establishment right here on the Big Island, as a silent-auction item to raise money for some charity back in 2000, where it was successfully bid on by a member of that establishment, name unknown at this point. But the name of that certain establishment . . .'

'Milt, you're not going to tell me it's the Royal Mauna Kea?'

'Bingo!' Milt said. 'Give that man a coconut.'

Nineteen

L ee was bushed. The ceremonial luncheon after the beat-the-pro event (Lynn had indeed beaten her on the front nine, but hadn't been able to overcome Lee's hole in one on the back nine); the awarding of prizes; the posing for photographs with contestants, and the general schmoozing that was expected of her had eaten up almost the entire afternoon. More than the time, though, the strain of being 'on' for eight straight hours had worn her out. Her smiling muscles, whatever they were called, were stretched so much they hurt.

But bushed or not, she was now absolutely engrossed, bent intently over the round glass patio table on which lay the copy of the Ancient and Honourable Oath, and admiringly listening to Peg run through her deductions.

Point by point, utilizing her flair for the dramatic to the full, Peg explained her reasoning as to its meaning. 'The End and the Beginning', 'the Heavens', 'Man's Ambrosial Shrine.'

'I don't really get that part,' Lee said. 'I mean, I think you're right – it has to be the upstairs bar – but you don't have to go *through* the bar to get to the library; you can walk in straight from the corridor, so why put it in there at all?'

Peg shrugged. 'Probably so the initiate could fortify himself with a quick single malt or two on the run, the way they seem to do with everything else around that place. Now, as I finally realized, the "Fount of All Wisdom" has to be—'

'The library. Yes of course! And the "Cavern of the Flames" has to be the fireplace in the library.' Lee's tiredness had evaporated. 'Peg, you're brilliant! Go ahead, I'm on tenterhooks here. What are tenterhooks, anyway? No, never mind. What's this . . . this Telamon and his brother? Could you make anything of that?'

'I could and did. First of all, I remembered that Telamon was the name of one of Jason's Argonauts.' At Lee's wrinkled brow, she added, 'You know, the Golden Fleece?'

'Oh, sure, the Golden Fleece,' Lee said as some schoolgirl memory stirred sluggishly in her brain. 'And the . . . the Calydonian bear – I think I mean *boar* – wasn't that in it somewhere?'

'You're right!' Peg said, no more amazed than Lee was. 'But then I thought, maybe there was something more to it than the old legend, so I looked it up in the big dictionary. And it turns out that "telamons" are male figures or busts used as support columns, or as decorative supports for doorways, lintels, fireplace mantels, or any other architectural feature that needs holding up.'

'Fireplace mantels!' Lee said, her anticipation growing. 'So there must be a pair of them supporting the mantel in the library – one on the south side and one on the north side of the fireplace! And you have to what? Unite them? Push them together?'

'Good girl,' said Peg. 'That's just what I came up with. So I got up and went back to the library.'

'And?'

'Well . . .' Peg reached for a coconut-crusted shrimp from the plate of *pupus* beside the oath and washed it down with a sip from her gin and tonic. 'Mmm.'

'And?' Lee said through gritted teeth.

'Lee, what do you think, shall I order some more *pupus*? Graham should be here any minute and we've pretty much scarfed them up, or rather, I have. Let me call room service—'

'Peg, forget the damn *pupus*! What happened when you went back to the library?'

'Oh, that. Well, there isn't any fireplace.'

'Isn't any . . . What do you mean, there isn't any?'

144

'I don't know how to put it any clearer than that, Lee. There. Is. No. Fireplace. In. The. Library. Nothing at all that could possibly be called the "Cavern of the Flames."'

With a groan, Lee sagged back in her chair. 'Well, why the heck didn't you tell me that in the first place?'

'I thought you'd enjoy the narrative suspense,' Peg said, and after looking blankly at each other for a couple of beats, they burst out laughing.

They were on Peg's patio at the hotel – a pleasant, spacious terrace outside her pleasant, spacious suite. (Lee's quarters, provided by the ever-frugal board of the Royal Mauna Kea, consisted of a standard double room on the second floor, with a standard little balcony, about which she was by no means complaining, but they were certainly no match for Peg's opulent, self-provided digs.) They had decided to have drinks and appetizers there, shielded from passers-by by a hedge of lusciously almond-scented poinsettia, but open to the songs of the strange tropical birds and to the soft booming of the distant surf. Graham would be there shortly, and Peg had ordered gin and tonic fixings and a combination *pupu* platter for all of them.

Relaxed now – feeling pretty chipper, in fact; Peg always had that effect on her – Lee squeezed another wedge of lime into her own gin and tonic, took a healthy swallow, and pried another nugget from the beef-and-pineapple skewer on her plate. 'So what's your conclusion?' she asked. 'Do you think you got the meaning wrong somehow?'

'No, I do not; not a chance. Everything fits too well, right up to the very last step.'

'Yes, but that last step's a real dilly,' Lee said. 'Without it, it all goes nowhere.'

'I can't argue with that.' She sighed. 'I'll try again tomorrow. You know me, Never-Give-Up Peggy.'

'Maybe I'll help you. I have a few odds and ends to take care of, but nothing serious until the luau and the glow-ball tournament tomorrow night. Thank goodness Wally doesn't expect me to play in it. He just wants me to be around for

145

the luau and be charming.' She shook her head. 'Golf in the dark,' she muttered. 'What's next, for God's sake?'

'Oh, it's—' Peg began.

'I know. Fun. I'd enjoy it.'

'Yes, you would, if you'd just lighten up a little. I mean, that's the point of things like this, isn't it? Fun? Not everybody is as serious about golf as you are. This is not exactly the US Open, you know.'

'You're right, Peg, of course you are. I've just had a little too much "fun" for one day today and I need to decompress for a while. I'll be raring to go by tomorrow night.'

'Sure you will. So how *did* your day go? Anybody beat you?'

'Using their handicaps, yes. Five or six of them. Some of the older ones are surprisingly good; Amory Aldrich and Evan Bunbury, in particular – or they would be if the yips hadn't gotten to them. Evan was club champion at sixteen, and I could see why. His swing is beautiful, even at eighty. So is Amory's for that matter, and he's even older. And Lynn Palakahela is terrific. She beat me straight out, no handicap, on the front nine.'

'Really? Is she that good?'

Lee smiled. 'I appreciate the compliment. And the answer is yes.' There was no reason to bring up Lee's 'accidental' miss on the first hole, and for her to mention it now would be petty. Anyway, Lynn *was* a heck of a golfer; it was surprising she'd never made it on the pro circuit. 'But aside from the golf, I had a pretty interesting day myself.'

Peg leaned forward. 'Ah, methinks I see a self-satisfied gleam in your eye. You've been doing some poking around, haven't you? Okay, what did you find out?'

'Peg, I have not been . . .' But of course she had, so she let it pass. 'I got a chance to ride with some interesting people, and, yes, I did learn a few things.'

She briefed Peg on what she'd heard from Lynn, from Grace, and from the three board members.

Peg listened avidly, without comment, until she'd finished.

'I can't believe Grace said all that to you,' she said when Lee was done. 'She was practically laying out the reasons she had for wishing her father dead.'

'Yes, I still don't know what to make of it. If she did actually kill him, why would she want to call attention to herself by spouting off about how much she hated him? For that matter, why would she be doing it if she *didn't* kill him? Either way, it would make anybody think she did. All I can think is that she's so bitter, so angry, over her father's marriage that her emotions took over. She just wasn't thinking logically. And the fact that her father was murdered just last night – by whoever – can't be doing anything for her mental stability right now.'

Peg looked carefully through the remaining appetizers on the platter, selected a tentacled chunk of fried calimari, dipped it in garlic mayonnaise, popped it delicately into her mouth, and chewed meditatively.

'I see it differently. What makes you think she isn't going around purposely trying to make herself look guilty so that you – well, not only you, but everybody, especially the police – are misled into thinking that since no guilty person would voluntarily go out of her way to make herself look that guilty, she must therefore be *not* guilty? What about that?'

Lee looked at her with something like awe. 'Peg, only you could come up with a scenario like that.'

'I know. I *am* brilliant, aren't I? But I believe I detected a certain amount of sarcasm in your tone just then. You don't think much of the idea?'

'Well, it is a little, um . . .'

'Over-elaborate? Rococo? Contrived?'

'"Dumb" is what I was going to say,' Lee said, laughing. 'Still, you can share the idea with Graham when he gets here and see what he thinks. But—'

'Graham *always* thinks my ideas are dumb.'

'No, he doesn't,' Lee said, truthfully enough. 'He thinks you're smart. But, actually, I'm more interested in the fact that only the board knew Hamish was going to walk them through the ritual of the oath. Nobody else.'

'I agree, that's interesting, but I'm not sure I see why it's so important.'

'You don't? Because it means that only four people – Lynn, Bernie, Evan, and Amory – knew he was going to do it, so—'

'Five people,' Peg corrected. 'Wally, too.'

'Oh, but Wally—'

'I know, I know, I don't think he killed anybody either. But you have to play this fair, Lee.'

Lee nodded her agreement. 'You're right, of course. Okay, five people. But that narrows it down a heck of a lot from two hundred, or however many people were there last night.'

'Which makes it more convenient, yes, except that we don't *know* that's why he was killed. It's like that old joke. A man is walking down a dark street and he sees this drunk crawling around on his hands and knees under a corner lamp post, and he asks him what he's looking for, and the drunk says he can't find his keys, and the man says, "I'll help you," and he starts looking too, but the drunk says, "Actually, I didn't lose them over here, I lost them over there, down in the middle of the block," so the man says, "Well, why are you looking for them here, then?" and the drunk looks at him as if he's stupid and says, "Because how am I supposed to find them over there? It's too dark."'

'Very funny. And your point is . . .?'

'My point is that just because it's more convenient to look in a certain place – or at a certain group of people – to find your answers, it doesn't mean that's where your answers are going to be.'

'But it's not only more convenient, Peg; it's logical. Everybody keeps wondering why Hamish was killed right then, right there in the clubhouse, where it was so risky. Why not before? Why not later? Well, isn't the obvious answer – and you're the one who pointed it out, for gosh sakes – that they wanted to stop him from explaining the ritual, and that that was their only chance to get him before he did?'

'Well, I know I said that, but now, with what you just told me, it doesn't seem to make sense. If the board members knew about it that morning, they had all day to do him in. They could have picked a better place and time. Heck, *any* place and time would have been better than that. Anyway, just because they were supposed to keep it secret doesn't mean they did. They could easily have told other people, which brings us back to your original two hundred.'

'Maybe they did, but maybe they didn't. It still seems like something worth keeping in mind.'

'Besides – and we've talked about this before – if nobody but Hamish knew what the ritual meant, how could they be afraid of it coming out? Of *what* coming out? I just have a hard time seeing it as a motive for murdering him.'

'Well, I sure don't,' Lee said stubbornly.

'Knock-knock,' said Graham from the side of the patio, where a Japanese-style, shoulder-high garden gate was set into the hedge. He opened it, clicked it shut behind him, and pulled up a third plastic lawn chair to join them.

'A motive for murdering him,' he mused to the open air as he sat down. 'Gee, I wonder what they're talking about.'

'Well, we learned some interesting things today,' Lee said gingerly.

'And we didn't do anything dangerous,' Peg added. 'Or silly. Now pour yourself a gin and tonic, have yourself some hors d'oeuvres—'

'What hors d'oeuvres?' Graham grumbled, but he wasn't doing too badly with what remained of the calimari and the chicken satay. He poured himself a gin and tonic to accompany it.

'And just listen for a while, okay? Then you can decide if we've been wasting our time or if it's worth passing along to Sergeant Fukuda.'

'I'll listen,' he said with a shake of his head, 'but I thought we'd agreed that you two were going to stay out of this and leave it to people who know what they're doing.'

'I don't remember agreeing,' Peg said blandly. 'I do seem to remember you *asserting* – rather overbearingly, if you'll allow me to say so – but I don't have any recollection of *agreeing*. Lee, dear, do you remember agreeing?'

Lee held up her hands. 'Leave me out of this one. I'm taking the Fifth. No comment at this time.'

Graham's sandy eyebrows knit, preparatory to the delivery of another scolding, but then they relaxed and dropped back into their usual handsome profile, and he laughed and drank some of his gin and tonic. 'Oh, the hell with it. I'd just be wasting my breath anyway.'

'I'll say this for him,' Peg said to Lee. 'The man is a slow learner, but he *does* eventually learn. Now then, here's what we found out.'

They repeated for him what they'd been talking about. Graham was supremely, disappointingly unimpressed – and said so. 'Sure, I'll pass it along to Milt; he'll probably find it interesting. He's into motives. But, truthfully, if it were my case, I wouldn't put too much in the way of resources into any of it. At least not yet.'

'Why not?' Peg demanded.

'Because, personally, I don't believe in this "motive" stuff.'

'I don't understand,' Lee said. 'How can you not believe in it? You've told me a hundred times how important it is in establishing a case.'

'In establishing a case, yes. It's hard to get a conviction without a convincing motive. But I don't believe in wasting time on it at this stage of an investigation. I don't really care why somebody killed somebody else; all I care about is whether he did or didn't. Look, Jimmy Hoffa's dead, and probably ten thousand people had a damn good motive for killing him, but so what? Where does it get you? There's no body, no evidence. Same kind of thing goes for Wyndham. If Milt started investigating everybody who didn't like the guy, he'd have to triple his staff, and even then, where would it get him?'

'So what *do* you do, then?' Peg huffed. 'If you don't believe in "this motive stuff," what are you supposed to believe in?'

'What I believe in is "this fact stuff,"' Graham said, smiling. 'I want evidence – physical, material data, not psychological conjecture.'

'Well, that's all fine and dandy, but you don't have any.'

'Ah, but we do,' Graham said complacently, and he told them about the letter from the Hui Malu Makuahine Pele group.

They listened, amazed. 'Somebody from the *club*?' Peg squeaked. 'A club member? But . . . but . . .'

'Are they sure it *was* a member that got the paper?' Lee asked. 'It couldn't have been an outsider?'

'No, it was a private affair, like everything else the Royal Mauna Kea does. They're not interested in opening their hallowed precincts to ordinary riff-raff. Besides that, the ink that was used on it turns out to be special-order stuff as well, made to a mid-nineteenth-century Indian ink formula. And the only place you're going to find it around here—'

'Is in the Royal Mauna Kea library,' Peg said slowly, 'in the inkwell next to the logbook, am I right?'

'Bingo!' said Graham, who knew a catchy phrase when he heard one. 'Give that lady a coconut.'

Twenty

The following day was perfection, at least until four P.M., by which time Lee was thoroughly, delightfully decompressed. The three of them had followed the plan they'd made two days before, which they'd had to postpone when the seemingly defunct horse race had been resuscitated. Peg had spent the day at the poolside, happily catching up with business and gossip on her laptop, while Graham and Lee had signed on with Cap'n Bob's Snorkelin', Swimmin', Scuba Divin' and Eatin' Cruises for a six-hour snorkeling jaunt. The boat, aptly named *Snorkeler's Bliss*, had anchored in a gorgeous little rock-rimmed bay, in ten feet of luminous, turquoise water. They had dog-paddled among wonderful coral-reef gardens for two hours, through shimmering schools of parrotfish, angelfish, and a thousand other incredibly colored tropical fish they couldn't even begin to name. On the way back to the Outrigger they had lunched on deck on the roast beef sandwiches, potato chips, and soft drinks that went along with the price.

Once back at the hotel, a delightfully drowsy and loose-limbed Lee had dozed for an hour, and then the three of them – Graham, Peg, and Lee – had driven to the club, where Graham was to meet with the board on their security concerns, and the two women repaired to the library to confront again the conundrum of the Ancient and Honourable Oath. Later on, they would meet again for the luau that was to precede the glow-ball tournament.

'Well, you're right about one thing,' Lee said. With nobody else in the library, she was able to speak at normal volume.

'What's that?' Peg said.

'There's definitely no fireplace in here.'

Peg snorted and shook her head. 'I really thought I had it. I mean, it seemed so obvious, so clear . . . The Fount of All Wisdom, the Cavern of the Flames . . .' She frowned. 'Wait a minute, just because there's no fireplace now doesn't mean there didn't used to be one. Maybe they blocked it up and covered it over.'

'Covered over a fireplace with sculpted heads of mythological Greek heroes? I wouldn't think so.'

'Well, it's worth a look,' she said, gazing around the room with narrowed eyes. 'I'm going to check and see if I can find any signs of replastering, or hollow spots in the walls.'

'You're still hoping to come up with your secret passage, aren't you?' Lee said, laughing.

'I wouldn't mind. You want to help? I can start going around this way, and you can go the other, and we'll see what we come up with.'

'No, I think I'll let you do that yourself,' Lee said. 'I want to have a look through the logbook. I just have a hunch that's where the answer is.'

'That's what I thought, and I practically went blind trying to find it. But go ahead, your eye is fresher. Maybe you'll see something I missed.'

'Can't hurt,' Lee said.

The book was open. She turned a sheaf of thick, heavy pages to get back to the beginning, then began leafing through them while Peg started around the room, energetically thumping the walls, like a doctor thumping a suspect chest cavity. Lee didn't have in mind a repetition of Peg's painstaking scrutiny of the previous day. She was, as Peg had said, taking advantage of her fresher eye, not *reading* – not exactly – but slowly turning the pages and letting them more or less flow across her vision, waiting for something to jump out at her.

About twenty pages in – at the page that held the original Ancient and Honourable Oath – something did. 'Peg,' she said slowly, 'weren't you under the impression that the oath went back to the very start of the club?'

Halfway round the room, Peg answered without pausing in her thumping, 'Hm? Yes, I suppose so.'

'Well, it didn't. The club opened on February eighth, 1905. The date on the oath is over three years later. "Commenced this first day of October, 1908."'

'Oh, yes, I guess I did notice that. I forgot. So?' She continued moving slowly, reaching between and around the books that lined the west wall to thump away at the plaster.

'Well, why do you think that is?'

'Who knows? Could be anything. Probably because nobody came up with it till then. Maybe there's no real reason, maybe it just—'

'No, I think there is a reason. I have the contract with Tiffany for the Cumberland Cup in front of me.'

Something – a slight tremble – in Lee's voice made Peg finally stop and turn around. 'And?'

'And the date of delivery is on it,' Lee said, barely breathing. 'October first, 1908. The very same day.'

They stared at each other. 'It's about the cup!' Peg cried. 'The Pride, the Honor, the Glory . . . the Cumberland Cup, the symbol of the club!'

Lee nodded gravely, barely able to keep from bursting into a shout herself. 'They used to hide it, remember? So the public didn't know where it was! But the club members, they'd want to know, wouldn't they? So couldn't the oath have been the key to where it was kept?'

Peg nodded excitedly along with her. 'You're a new member, you're given the oath to follow, and when you come to the end of it—'

'The secret hiding place of the cup is revealed to you! That's your reward. Peg, that's it!'

Peg had come up to see the Tiffany contract for herself, and had then leafed forward again to the oath and stood re-reading it for a few seconds. 'Houston, we have a problem.'

'No fireplace, you mean. No Telamon. Well, we can work

on that. We'll figure it out. I'd say we're doing pretty well so far.'

'No, it isn't that,' Peg said, scowling down at the oath. 'There's something else that doesn't quite add up. Look at the first question and answer: "Whose is it? Yours and yours alone." How can that refer to the Cumberland Cup? The new member's just one person. It can't be his and his alone. It belongs to the whole club.'

'Oh, I see what you mean.'

'Well, don't look so dejected. I think you're right. I just think there's something we don't quite understand yet.'

But Lee couldn't help being dejected. She'd thought she'd had it figured out, but Peg was right. How could 'yours and yours alone' refer to the cup? It didn't make sense. She stretched, took a deep breath, and went back to browsing through the logbook while Peg took up her thumping where she'd left off.

Forty minutes later, Lee had come to the end of the book without result. She sighed and began turning the pages backward, from the end toward the front, in hopes that something small that she'd missed might be more likely to catch her eye. When she came again to a full-page color photograph of the Cumberland Cup itself, she paused to look at it – it really was a beautiful thing – and moved on, but a few pages later she froze.

'Peg!'

Peg, having finished her fruitless search for the disappearing fireplace, was slumped in a chair at one of the library tables, moping. Lee's sudden call startled her upright. 'Huh? What?'

'Come over here!' Lee said, flipping pages until she got back to the photograph of the cup. 'Look at this!' she cried. 'It was staring right at us!'

Peg peered at the picture for a good twenty seconds. '*What's* staring right at us?'

'Well, what do you see?'

'What do I see? I see the Cumberland Cup.'

'And?'

'You mean in the background? I don't know, there's a—'

'No, not the background,' Lee said, laughing. 'Look at the cup itself. What's on it?'

'On it?' She was getting a little irritated now. 'Well, I guess that's the famous Mana Stone there, and . . .' She studied it another moment. 'Oh my,' she said softly. 'There's our answer.'

Around the neck of the urn-shaped Cumberland Cup was a red-white-and-blue ribbon from which depended a pewter medallion with a bas-relief of palm trees and mountains. It was the medallion given to new members of the Royal Mauna Kea.

'I think so,' Lee said with deep satisfaction. 'When the initiate completed the last step, uniting Telamon and his brother, whatever that means, he found the cup – the Pride, the Honor, the Glory – looking exactly like this, and around it hung his own personal medallion, inscribed with his very own name – His and His Alone.'

'By George, I think she's got it,' Peg sang in a whisper, then laughed. 'And you said *I* was brilliant.'

Lee flushed with pleasure. 'Oh, I was just lucky. It just—'

'No, you weren't *just* anything. I pored over this stuff for hours yesterday, and I didn't get this far.' She shook her head. 'It's the cup all right, that's what it's about.'

They were silent for a while, looking down at the photograph and pondering, and then Peg spoke again. 'Look at this thing, will you? A solid silver urn. Diamonds, rubies, onyx . . . people have been murdered for a lot less. Lee, this is all starting to hang together. Everybody's been wondering for years where the cup is. Well, what if it's been right here in the clubhouse, in its secret niche, or passageway, or whatever, all this time, and Hamish was killed to keep him from revealing that? When he walked them through the oath?'

'I don't know, Peg . . .' Lee began.

'And if that's so, then the chances are good that it had to be one of the board members, right? If you're right about

156

them being the only ones who knew he was going to do it?'

'I don't know, Peg. I mean, I think we're right about the cup, but I can't quite get a handle on the logic of it. There are so many questions. There's the old problem: if he was the only one who understood what it meant, how would anyone know it had to do with the cup at all? And then, why would someone kill Hamish to keep him from telling about it anyway? What conceivable good could it do them? And what the heck is Telamon and where is he? Or it? And where's the *fireplace*? And . . .'

Peg blew out her cheeks, exhaled, and sank back into one of the chairs. 'The more answers we get, the more questions we wind up with. Are you sure it's supposed to work that way?'

Twenty-One

Graham's session with the board to discuss security problems started out on the rocky side, but they became
markedly more fond of him when they understood that he
was neither charging them for his time this afternoon nor
offering his own services for hire. There were several
reputable security system providers located in Hawaii, certi-
fied by the International Association of Professional Security
Consultants, and one of them, Safeguard Systems, was located
right there in Kona. Working through a local outfit like
Safeguard, he told them, would cost a lot less and be a lot
simpler than working with a mainland consultant like
Graham.

They fell even more in love with him when he told them
that, in his opinion, creating and maintaining a physical
security system for the 6,800-yard golf course would be
infinitely more expensive, time consuming, and prone to
glitches than simply resigning themselves to living with the
existence of the diggers and repairing the holes when they
found them. Only Wally gave up a soft, resigned sigh when
he heard this.

As for the clubhouse itself, however, that was a different
proposition. There, especially considering the many valuable
objects it contained, they were overdue for some kind of
integrated electro-mechanical security set-up that included
access control, intrusion detection, and interactive, 'intelligent' CCTV video systems. That all sounded expensive (and
was), but he explained that they could save quite a bit of
money by doing much of their own initial site analysis – and

that, in fact, he had prepared a checklist for them that they were welcome to use.

The rest of the meeting was devoted to the nitty-gritty contents of the checklist and how to gather and prepare the necessary data: the number and location of windows and doors; condition of windows, doors, and locks; identification of doors used for deliveries, services, and/or employee traffic; equipment and objects requiring special protection; procedures for dealing with ex-employees' access; outside lighting of vulnerable areas, and on, and on, and on.

By the time they were done, a forceful, authoritative Lynn had designated each of the board members responsible for specific categories of the checklist, and poor Wally had been delegated enough work to keep him busy for the rest of the year. Still, he seemed happy with the way it had gone – or happy, at any rate, that something was at last being done. After the board had left, Graham stayed in the meeting room with Wally to answer his questions and to go over some of the items in more detail.

As a result, Graham didn't leave the boardroom for another thirty minutes, and so he was surprised to find Bernie Gottschalk sitting on a sofa in the Grand Foyer, pretending to look at a copy of *Fortune* magazine, but keeping one eye on the boardroom door and very obviously waiting for him.

'Oh, hey, Graham, got a minute?' he said, jumping up. He was doing his best to look casual, as if he'd accidentally happened to spot Graham, but he was doing a poor job.

'Sure,' Graham said, stopping.

Bernie looked over each shoulder. There were a few other members in the foyer, chatting or looking at newspapers, and others in the downstairs bar only a few yards away. Apparently they were too close.

'Would you mind going outside, taking a walk or something? I don't like to talk in here.'

Graham's interest grew. This wasn't about security systems. 'You bet. Let's go.'

They went out the front door, and since the luau would

soon be starting on the east terrace, so that nobody was teeing off on the first hole, they strolled on to the first fairway itself and down toward the green. Whatever Bernie had to say to him, he wanted to be as far away as they could get from anyone who could possibly overhear. They walked a good hundred yards down the fairway, with Graham biding his time, before Bernie said anything.

'Well, I guess I better get it off my chest,' he mumbled.

'I guess you'd better.'

Bernie stopped walking, pulled a pack of cellophane-wrapped cigars from his shirt pocket, fiddled with them, crinkling the cellophane, and put them absent-mindedly back in his pocket without opening them. 'Listen, you know those letters the board has been getting from that cult?'

Graham nodded.

'I can tell you who wrote them.' He waited for Graham's reaction.

'Why tell me? You should be telling Sergeant Fukuda.'

'Fukuda scares me. He's not as . . . as accessible as you are. I figured you could pass it on to him.'

'I don't think so. If it makes you feel any better, I can go with you to see him. We could do it right now.'

Bernie's face clouded. 'No, I don't want to go see him,' he snapped. 'I already told you he . . . hell, do you want to know who wrote them or not?'

'I already know who wrote them,' Graham said.

Bernie stopped and turned to face him with a challenging scowl. 'Like hell you do. Who did?'

'You,' Graham said.

For the first couple of miles on the twenty-minute highway drive from the Royal Mauna Kea to Fukuda's office, Bernie sat slumped and listless in the passenger seat, looking as if he'd already been tried and condemned, and had just heard the news that his appeal had been rejected.

Graham glanced over at him. 'Buckle your seat belt,' he said.

Bernie complied as if in a trance, but the motion seemed to bring him to life a little. 'How did you know?' he asked apathetically.

I knew because it was written all over your face, you poor sap, Graham thought. All that body language – waffling, fidgeting, hemming and hawing. What else could it mean?

'We know,' he said omnisciently, to put the fear of God into him.

Graham doubted very much that Bernie had killed anyone, but he'd come around to thinking that the cup was involved in some way, and the more candid Bernie was about what he knew, the better. If nothing else, he could help eliminate some false leads that Fukuda might be following. And apprehension and self concern, Graham had learned over the years, were highly effective stimulants for candor.

'Don't you want to hear the rest of it?' Bernie asked.

Graham mimed a shrug of unconcern. 'I can wait till we get there.'

Bernie made a pathetic little *urping* noise, like a dog that had just realized that whatever he'd gobbled down so hungrily a moment ago didn't agree with him, and sank back into his funk.

'I didn't kill him!'

'We heard you the first time,' Fukuda said.

And the second, Graham thought, *and the third*.

They were in one of the interrogation rooms at the Kona police station – Graham, Fukuda, and Bernie at the table, a detective taking notes in the far corner of the room, and, for good measure, a tape recorder whirring softly away on the table. And a very pleasant room it was, as interrogation rooms went. Unsoiled carpet, windows looking east toward the distant, green mountains, clean, peach-colored walls with decorations – a blow-up photograph of camellia blossoms, another of a sunset on the Kohala Coast, a poster for the 2004 Parker Ranch rodeo in Waimea, a calendar with a picture of Akaka Falls – and no sign anywhere of a one-way glass. The gleaming wooden furniture was a nice touch too, a long way from the typical chipped Formica table and old olive-green metal chairs. Even the usual prisoner smell – of perspiration, fear and dirty clothes – was missing. All in all, Graham thought, it was more like an agreeable little conference room than an interrogation chamber.

None of which, however, did anything to soften Fukuda's steely, relentless questioning, or to soothe Bernie's obvious discomfort.

'So how about explaining again just what the point of it all was?' Fukuda said.

'I already told you a hundred times!' Bernie cried. 'You got it on the damn tape.'

'You also told us a hundred times you didn't kill anybody,' Fukuda said calmly. 'That doesn't seem to stop you from telling us again.'

Bernie sighed. 'You suppose I could get another cup of coffee?'

'Absolutely.'

Without being told, the detective left to get it and Bernie went wearily through his story one more time. Yes, he had written all three of the letters that had been received by the club over the past few months. No, there was no such thing as the Hui Malu Makuahine Pele cult. He had made the name up. There was only him. No, he hadn't been responsible for any of the digging; only the letters. And the letters had been a joke, he insisted; he was just jerking Hamish's chain, that was all.

'Because he blackballed you when you first tried to join,' Fukuda said.

'Well, not only—'

'And opposed your election to the board.'

'I did *not* kill that man,' Bernie said stolidly, accepting a cardboard cup of watery machine coffee from the returning detective. 'Why would I want to do that? I'd have to be crazy. What good would it do me?'

'And did it work?' Fukuda asked. 'Did it jerk Hamish's chain?'

'Yeah, it irritated him.' He smiled just a little. 'And then I got a kick out of listening to old Amory pontificate about them.' His voice lowered to an imitation of Amory Aldrich's slow, solemn speech. 'My travels have taken me to many exotic places, and I have seen many a strange and curious—'

'What made you use that particular paper?' Graham asked. Fukuda had told him to jump in whenever he felt like it, but until now he'd simply observed.

'Well, I won it at this auction and it was supposed to be old paper, from, like, a hundred years ago, so I thought – I don't know, it seemed to fit.'

'And the ink? The same reason?'

'Yeah, the same reason.'

'Weren't you concerned that they'd be recognized? Or that somebody would remember you as the successful bidder on the paper?'

'No, why would anybody remember something like that? It was five years ago. Why would they even make the connection?' He sipped and grimaced. 'Jesus, this coffee sucks.'

'You weren't worried that the police would be able to trace the ink, the paper?'

'No, I wasn't worried. I knew we'd never go to the police with that stuff. And if we did, why would the police go to that kind of trouble over a couple of crank letters?'

'But we did,' Fukuda said.

'Yeah, because somebody murdered Hamish. But—'

'It wasn't you,' Fukuda finished for him.

'That's exactly right. Look, do I need a lawyer? Am I under arrest or something?'

Fukuda pushed back from the table. He was tired too. 'Not at this point. You can take off now. Thanks for your co-operation, Mr Gottschalk.'

Bernie hesitated before getting up. 'Sergeant . . . I realize now how dumb this all was, and what an idiot it makes me look like. Does it have to come out?'

'I'm not gonna broadcast it.'

'Thank you.'

'But I'm not gonna hide it either.'

Bernie made his sick-dog sound again and put his hand to his forehead.

'Come on, Bernie, I'll drive you back,' Graham said.

Twenty-Two

The luau preceding the glow-ball tournament was uneventful but not unpleasant, except in that Graham had disappointingly failed to appear. But there wouldn't really have been much time to spend with him anyway. Lee, as the 'celebrity' guest, presented prizes for the indoor putting championship and the horse race, then posed for pictures with the winners, signed a few autographs (still a new-enough phenomenon with her to make her feel like an impostor doing it), and more or less played the part of the celebrity she was supposed to be.

By that time the banana-leaf-wrapped pig, which had been roasting in its covered, stone-lined pit since before noon, was ready, and everyone sat down to eat at tables that had been arranged in long lines on the flagstone terrace. There were roasted yams, pineapples, and bananas to go with it, along with hot dogs, hamburgers, chicken, and fish for those who weren't keen on digging gobbets out of a whole pig that was grinning back at you as you did it (Lee was among this minority, although she accepted a small piece for the sake of politeness), and coconut and pineapple pie for dessert.

After a meal like that, Lee felt as if she'd have a hard time making it through two holes of miniature golf, but when the last of the sun disappeared into the sea and Wally announced that the glow-ball tournament would begin in fifteen minutes, there was a flurry of excitement as participants bustled into their carts and got rolling. With something like a hundred and fifty people signed up, there was going to be a 'shotgun start,' meaning that two foursomes would tee off from each of the eighteen holes and work their way around the course from there, all beginning at the same time, when the shotgun (actually a starter's pistol) was fired by Wally and heard across the grounds.

Lee too felt a small ripple of excitement run through her. She had been on pins and needles, expecting that at any moment Wally would ask her to join a foursome, or act as marshal, or do anything else related to this wacky event, but he had yet to do so. And now it looked as if she was going to get away with it!

But as she stood with Wally, Peg, and a few of the members, she saw three women approaching, two of them middle-aged and one of them not much more than a child, all with their eyes bashfully but very definitely on her, and her heart sank.

'Wally?' One of the adults began in an arch, schoolgirl's voice. 'Molly isn't feeling quite herself—'

'It was all that coconut pudding,' the youngster said, laughing and blowing out her cheeks.

'So we're down to a threesome, and we were hoping that, well . . .'

Again three pairs of eyes moved invitingly in Lee's direction, and her heart dropped a little further south, to somewhere around her ankles. There was no way out of this. Golf in the dark – wth balls that lit up! Good God! She was, however, working up a surprised smile of acceptance, worthy of a gracious celebrity, when Peg, good old dependable Peg, stepped brightly in and saved her.

'Are you looking for someone to round out your foursome? Well, if Wally could find me a set of loaners—'

'No problem.'

'—then I'd absolutely adore it.' Lee sent her a look of gratitude, although the eager expression on Peg's face showed that it was no sacrifice on her part. She really would love it. Each to her own, Lee thought wonderingly.

'Oh, *marvelous*,' the first woman enthused, more or less

successfully masking her disappointment. 'You're Peg, I know. I remember you from the putting championship. I'm Linda Dow, and this is Maggie Browne, and this is—'

'I'm Emily LaLonde,' the girl announced, sticking out a hand to be shaken. She was no more than fourteen, and skinny at that, but brimming with adolescent self-confidence.

Peg shot Lee an inquisitive glance as she shook Emily's hand, meaning: *It's all right if I go? You don't mind being on your own for the next few hours?*

Lee responded with a near-imperceptible shake of her head. She was fine. She would, in fact, rather have spent the evening watching her fingernails grow than chasing glowing golf balls over the fairways, but as it was, she wouldn't have to. Graham had called her cell phone not long before, to say that although he'd gotten tied up with Sergeant Fukuda, he'd be along soon, and would she save him a slice of coconut pie?

Go enjoy yourself, I'm fine, she thought-transferred to Peg.

She had snared a slice of the pie for Graham, and a couple of hot dogs as well, in case he hadn't had any dinner at all, and was coming back to chat with Wally, when another woman, considerably older and notably more imperious than the three who had just left with Peg, came up to him with 'complaint' clearly stamped across her forehead.

'Wallace, you're always doing this. Rush, rush, rush. Fifteen minutes is scarcely sufficient time to freshen up and get out to our assigned tees. And you've put me at thirteen, for goodness sake, clear on the other side of the course. You couldn't have put me farther away if you'd tried.'

'I'm sorry about that, Mrs Bancroft. The assignments were done randomly—'

'Yes, and there are all too many things around here that are done randomly, if you want my opinion. If at least you'd thought to locate the ladies' lounges on the main floor when you so very big-heartedly opened this establishment to women, it might—'

'Mrs Bancroft, that was done in 1965. I had nothing to

do with it. Believe me, if it was up to me, I'd have had them downstairs.'

She peered severely at him for a moment, then turned on her heel and stomped toward the clubhouse. 'A likely story,' Lee heard her mutter.

Watching her go, Wally shook his head. 'What a life. You know, if she'd just headed up to the ladies' room without stopping to chew me out for something that happened when I was fifteen years old, she could have been out on number thirteen by now, taking her practice swings. But no, she has to . . . Lee, is something wrong?'

'What? Oh, no.' She realized that she had absently put the food on a nearby table and had been staring intently into the middle distance, replaying Mrs Bancroft's words and paying no attention whatsoever to Wally. 'Sorry, I was just . . . A thought just occurred to me. Wally, do you happen to have the plans for the clubhouse?'

'Sure. There are blueprints in my office for the wiring, the plumbing—'

'No, not the current plans, the old ones, the original ones, the ones from before 1965.'

He frowned. 'I suppose we've got 'em stowed away some-where. Why do you want them?'

'Do you have any idea where?'

'Not really. I can hunt them up for you tomorrow. What do you need them for?'

'You don't think you could find them tonight? Now?'

'No, I wouldn't know where to look. Anyway, I should be out at the glow-ball thing with everybody else.' He thought for a moment. 'I bet the originals are in the logbook, though.'

'No, they're not. There are just the architect's sketches of the outside. Rats.' She chewed on her lip, then brightened. 'But on the other hand . . .' she murmured to herself.

'Well, what's so important about them, anyway?'

But she was already on her way toward the clubhouse entrance. 'Wally,' she called over her shoulder, 'don't let them clear those hot dogs and that pie away; they're for Graham.'

'Okay,' he yelled after her rapidly retreating figure. 'But why do you—?' He shrugged good-humoredly. 'Ah, the hell with it.'

Twenty-Three

Had there been an observer in the library to see her, she would have seemed as calm as a marble statue, standing so quietly in front of the stand that held the logbook, but inside, her heart was pounding away. She was as excited as a puppy at a picnic. How could the idea have failed to occur to her, or to Peg? It was so very obvious! And it was there all along, for her to see.

Maybe the problem was that it was *too* obvious. It should have struck her when Peg failed to find the fireplace in the library. It should have struck her when Lynn made a passing reference to the ladies' card room, locker room, and lounge that had been installed when women were first admitted to the club. But at last – and it was about time – it *did* strike her when Mrs Bancroft grumbled about the location of the women's restroom.

It was so very simple: if they had had to create all those new rooms in the existing structure, then, clearly, the original floor plan must have been drastically altered, and many rooms would have had to be modified, or reduced in size, or shifted, or converted to other functions to make space for the requirements of the feminine invasion.

So, the pre-1965 library – the Fount of All Wisdom, the library of Mr Babbington's on-again, off-again memory – was not the room in which Lee now stood. The old library, or rather the room in which it had been housed, with its Cavern of the Flames and its twin Telamon brothers, was still there, all right; it was just somewhere else.

Simple. Obvious.

She was leaning over the logbook now, studying the original renderings of the clubhouse's exterior to double check the placement of the chimneys (and thus the fireplaces). A few minutes earlier, after a first look at the drawings, she had gone outside and circled the building to make sure that there had been no additions tacked on to the structure as a whole. There hadn't. Whatever changes had been made had been made to the inside alone.

The building had four external stone chimneys, each running from the ground to the roof. Assuming that each housed two fireplaces, one per floor, that was a total of eight, some of which she had seen but not really noticed. Looking at the renderings, she determined that the upstairs ones would be in the smoking room, the private dining room, the billiards room, and the women's card room. The smoking room, which she had never been in, was next to the library (the library of today), so she began her hunt for the twin Telamons there.

The spacious, handsome room, easily big enough to have once been the library, was silent and deserted, like the rest of the building, but through the open French doors she could hear laughter, some of it distinctly tipsy (alcohol had flowed freely at the luau), floating up from the nearby fairways as people chased their illuminated golf balls around the course. The laughter, muted and made other-worldly by distance and by the heavy, perfumed air of the Hawaiian night, sent shivers down her spine and added to her excitement. It was strange, though, how the blazing chandeliers throughout the clubhouse made it seem emptier, spookier, than it would have been if at least some of the vacant rooms had been dark.

The huge fireplace, as expected, was on the west wall. The small bronze plaque beside it read *Schloss Steinhausen, 17th c., Darmstadt, Germany*, and the façade was so crowded with sculpted reliefs that she thought she'd hit pay dirt on the very first try. However, a closer look showed that the bristling figures were all animals – stags, lions, bears, dogs. Nothing that could conceivably have been a Telamon, and no twin anythings to 'unite,' although she tried, pushing on everything that stuck out in every direction she could, all to no avail.

The private dining room was next. Here, the fireplace was of black cast iron, and the low reliefs were of urns and flowers. No soap.

In the women's card room, the fireplace was fronted with beautiful, veined marble – no sculptures at all. From there she went downstairs. Four more fireplaces, four more strike-outs.

That left one to go, back on the upper floor, but she hesitated at the foot of the stairway, steeling herself, before going to look. Something in her had known from the start that that was where the search was going to end up, but instead of starting there, she had put it off, hoping that her instincts were wrong. Given her druthers, she'd prefer never, ever, to enter that room again.

The Christopher Porthmellon Billiards Room – the room where Hamish Wyndham's body had been found. She'd been there only that one time, and she hadn't had the time or inclination to notice whether there even was a fireplace, let alone what it looked like.

She went slowly up the ornate staircase, wondering if she ought to wait until later, when she could have Peg with her, or better yet Graham – or better yet Peg *and* Graham – but she brushed aside this thought as unworthy. There was no reason to be frightened, and anyway, she wasn't frightened, she was just a little spooked, that's all. Understandable under the circumstances, but not any less childish for that.

Still, when she got to the closed door, she hesitated again. The last time she had reached for this door handle it had been pulled open by a gray-faced Lynn Palakahela, behind whom, at the foot of a massive pool table, an even grayer-faced Hamish Wyndham, covered in his own blood, had lain on the carpeted floor.

Lynn was out on the golf course now, and Hamish was . . . wherever he was. She knew those things, naturally – knew them for facts – and yet she was gripped with the crazy expectation that when she did finally open the door she would find the very same awful scene waiting for her.

'Crazy expectation is right,' she muttered to herself. 'Don't be an idiot.' She pressed down the handle, resisted the impulse to shut her eyes, flung the door open, and stepped firmly into the room.

Empty. Her breath, which she hadn't realized she'd been holding, came fluttering weakly out of her. *Well, of course it was empty, dummy. What did you expect?*

She looked cautiously about her. One of the things she'd been qualmish about seeing, she realized now, was the bloodstain; the blood from Hamish's crushed head that had soaked so deeply and blackly into the otherwise spotless saffron carpet. But there wasn't any bloodstain. There wasn't any carpet, either. (Of course; she should have remembered that the police had taken it away.) Not even a carpet pad, just the beautiful old oak flooring. The ornate koa-wood molding that they'd had to pry up to get at the carpet now leaned against the wall in four-foot lengths, but everything else that was movable or detachable had been taken away: the chairs, the pool table, the cue rack, the wall hangings, the drapes. Only a second pool table, shoved forlornly into a corner, remained.

That, and the marble fireplace on the far wall. The moment she saw it, she knew she'd found what she was looking for. Yesterday morning she'd never heard of telamons. Tonight, she recognized them instantly: two bearded male figures, each about three feet tall, that stood on the mantel, holding up a second mantel above them. The figures, nude except for a twist of sculpted cloth, held up by means mysterious and invisible, that reached around from the side and tactfully hid certain portions of their anatomy from view, were most definitely twins, though done in reverse. A little over two feet apart, the one on the left faced partly to his right and held up the second mantel with his left arm; the one on the right faced partly to his left and supported the mantel with his right arm.

A little intense calculation (she'd never been good with direction) told her that the fireplace was on the east wall of the room. That meant the figure on the left was Great Telamon of the North, the one on the right his twin of the South.

This was it, all right. It had to be.

She approached them almost respectfully, as if they were indeed figures of Greek legend. Blank faced and serene, they stared off in their respective directions with their pupil-less eyes, carrying their load easily, looking *extremely* immoveable. And an examination, with eyes and fingers, confirmed their immovability. They weren't free standing, as she'd first thought, but securely attached – cement? concrete? – to the heavy marble slab behind them, six feet wide and four feet high, that ran the length of the fireplace. How was anybody supposed to 'unite' them? They were impossible to move.

Not that that stopped her from trying. She pushed, she pulled – she even whacked them with her open hand. Nothing happened. Baffled and perspiring, with a throbbing right hand (out of frustration she'd whacked them harder than she'd intended to), she stepped back a couple of paces to perhaps gain some new perspective from distance. And she did. She noticed that the six-foot marble slab was actually composed of three individual, two-foot-wide slabs, one behind each figure, and one in the middle, separated by hairline seams. Was it the slabs that moved, and not the figures themselves?

She went ferociously at the slabs behind the figures. Again, nothing. They couldn't have been more solidly in place. Could this *not* be the right fireplace? Could she and Peg have misunderstood the oath entirely?

'Impossible,' she said aloud, and to the figures she said, 'You're starting to irritate me.'

She laid a hand against the center slab, thinking of it as a kind of warning to the fireplace as a whole. *Don't think I'm finished with you yet, pal.*

There was the slightest clicking sound, and with it a kind of vibration. Had it moved? She pushed harder against it.

She got both hands into the act and leaned her body into it.

And it moved. It gave. The center slab slid back a couple of inches. Startled, Lee jumped back. The slab in the middle was now, in effect, recessed two inches, relative to the slabs at either end – the ones bearing the telamons. That meant that, with the center slab out of the way, it was possible for them to be pushed up against one another.

If, that is, they could be moved.

She gave it a try, reaching out to put one hand on each of the figure's forward knees, and pulling. When they didn't move, she took a breath and pulled harder. The slab on the left remained stuck fast, but the other one, the slab that bore the Telamon of the North, shifted! Under Lee's pressure, it rode over some kind of hump or catch and then, freed, glided easily on its own toward the other, rumbling above the fireplace opening as if on rollers, until it bumped up against the far slab with a solid, rewarding *clack*. The twin Telamons were united!

Lee stood stock still, again holding her breath, staring hard at nothing, focusing her attention on her hearing, waiting for some unseen door to creak open on rusty hinges, or maybe even for the entire fireplace to slowly rotate on its hidden axis, revealing the secret passage that was so dear to Peg's heart.

The seconds dragged by. No door, no secret passage, no nothing. Well, what the heck . . . ? She let out her breath and looked up, and when she did, she found herself looking straight at the Cumberland Cup. When the slab had slid over to the opposite side of the fireplace, it had revealed a richly paneled recess in the wall behind it, and it was in this recess that the celebrated, century-old symbol of the Royal Mauna Kea – the fabled cup that had supposedly been lost for more than sixty years – stood, its splendor only slightly dimmed by the crumpled, filthy tarpaulin that draped its top. Respectfully, she removed the cloth – some kind of old sack, she realized; something that had been used for transporting it from place to place in the old days – and laid it aside, brushing dust from the cup's rim and shoulder. She stepped back. Pristine and perfect, the exquisite urn glowed softly in the light from the chandeliers. Stuck into a corner behind it were three pieces of wood: the broken pool cue, the murder weapon. She made an effort not to look at them.

She had anticipated exultation, but instead came a flood of questions. Had the cup never been 'lost' at all, had it been right here all along? And if so, why had the club claimed that it had vanished in the first place? And why had Hamish kept it to himself all these years? Why, for that matter, had so many others, now gone, kept the secret until their deaths? And if someone had killed Hamish to keep him from revealing it (by now, she was almost certain this was the case), then *why* had they killed him? What had they possibly hoped to gain that was worth murder? And—

But now the exultation broke through. The questions could wait for Graham and Sergeant Fukuda. She patted the cup on its shoulder the way she might pat an old friend on the shoulder. 'Gotcha,' she breathed, looking keenly forward to the expression on Peg's face when she brought her here to see what they had jointly succeeded in discovering. For it was most definitely a joint discovery – more Peg's than hers, really. Peg had made the critical connections. Lee had merely put the final couple of pieces together. And what about Graham, what would he say? And Sergeant Fukuda?

A soft sound, or perhaps some slight change in the air pressure, as if a window or door had been opened or shut, sent a shiver trickling up her spine. Was someone in the room with her? She turned . . .

Struggling back from oblivion – swimming up, and up, and up, out of a bottomless void – nauseated and panicking, her heart racing, she awoke with a gasp and found herself sprawled on her back in still, utter darkness. She thought at first that a mask of some thick, heavy fabric – wool, velvet, flannel – was wrapped around her head, cutting off sight, and sound, and air. Her fingers scrabbled desperately at her cheeks, trying to tear it off. But there was nothing there, only the impenetrable blackness, so thick and tangible it seemed not to be out there, but pressed like a curtain up against her face.

Am I blind? she thought in a daze. She put her left wrist, with its luminescent watch, to her eyes. There, to her relief, was the familiar, friendly little circle of green numerals. *No, not blind.* She moved her arms, her legs, her fingers. Everything seemed to work. *Not blindfolded, not blind, not bound, not seriously injured, not being threatened by anybody, as far as she could tell. All right then, calm down. Think.*

She made herself lie back against the hard, flat surface – a wooden floor it was, old and splintery – and take a few deep, steady breaths. In. Out. Once, twice, three times. Slowly, the thumping in her chest began to subside, the nausea receded, and something nearing lucid thought began to flow along the pathways of her brain. *Think. What happened? How did I get here? Where is 'here'?*

The cup, she thought, as bits of memory filtered back in bright, broken little shards. *I'd found the cup!* And even now, bewildered and frightened as she was, the recollection brought a thrill of victory with it. *I was standing in front of it, I was looking at it, and . . . and . . .*

But that was all she could remember, and even that seemed far away and not altogether real. The throbbing, stinging ache on the side of her head, beside her left eye, was real enough, though, and a touch of her fingers confirmed that she'd been struck there. The skin was tender and swelling, but not broken. There wasn't any blood and there didn't seem to be any underlying damage to her skull; she hoped not, anyway. *Oh, brother*, she thought, not altogether pertinently, *am I going to have to get married with an egg-sized lump on my face and maybe even, God forbid, a black eye?*

All right, get back to the here and now, she told herself. *Obviously, somebody slugged me and then brought me here and left me. That's what must have happened. But when?*

How long have I been here? How long have I been uncon-scious? She raised her watch to a few inches from her eyes again. Eight thirty-five. She'd left Wally to go up to the library at about eight, so that meant – assuming that it wasn't eight thirty-five in the morning – that whatever had happened, she couldn't have been out for more than five minutes; perhaps only two or three.

As to where exactly she was, there were no sounds, no smells (except the damp, gritty smell of stone), no vibra-tions, nothing to provide a clue, but it didn't take that much imagination to figure out.

She had found Peg's secret passage for her. The hard way.

Twenty-Four

Emily LaLonde, whom Peg had assumed was one of the other women's daughters, but wasn't, turned out to be the best golfer of their foursome by a country mile. Not only that, she was the best female golfer in the entire club; the reigning women's champion. And also, as she proudly and damn near incessantly proclaimed (if there were a women's chatterbox champion, Emily would be a shoo-in for that title too), she was the youngest full-fledged member in the history of the Royal Mauna Kea, inasmuch as it was a long-standing rule that those who won the championship, whatever their ages, were automatically granted full membership. And she had only been *thirteen* when she'd won and advanced from family membership to full membership on her own. That old Mr Aldrich had said it was ridiculous to have thirteen-year-old full members and wanted to change the rules, but Mr Wyndham said that the rules were the rules, whether you liked them or not, and so here she was. And her sister Sybil was an even better golfer than *she* was, believe it or not, and Sybil was only eleven. . .

By the time their foursome finished up, Peg's ears were sore, and she was glad to make her getaway. At the same time, the girl's non-stop babbling had set in motion the wheels of a new and intriguing idea, so that as soon as they'd all said goodbye and told each other how much fun it'd been, she headed for the clubhouse, looking for Lee and thinking that she might be in Wally's office.

She wasn't. Wally was sitting out on the moonlit terrace with Graham (who was shoveling in coconut pie and milk),

179

but neither of them had seen Lee for a while.

'She's in the clubhouse somewhere,' Wally said. 'When you find her, get her out of there, will you? I'd like to lock up and go home. I'm beat.'

'Will do.'

She checked the obvious places – the library and restroom – and when she didn't find her she stood out in the open area on the second floor, above the grand foyer, and bellowed her name. There was no answer. The place was so empty it echoed. Puzzled, but with no reason to worry, she shrugged and went back to the library, back to the great logbook of the Royal Mauna Kea, to see if she could find the answers to a couple of fresh questions that the voluble Emily had unknowingly stirred up.

It didn't take long. Inside of a minute, she found the faded old *Coast Times* newspaper clipping she was looking for.

FAMED CUP VANISHES

A spokesman for the Royal Mauna Kea Golf and Country Club confirmed to this newspaper today that the magnificent Cumberland Cup, the bejeweled trophy created by the great Louis Comfort Tiffany, has vanished from the club's premises and is presumed stolen. The police have been informed and are now pursuing . . .

But she wasn't interested in what the police had been pursuing, or in anything else about the story. It was the date she was after, and that had been obligingly inked in for her by some presumably long-dead hand, in the upper right-hand corner of the clipping: December 13, 1941.

'Ha!' Peg said aloud, as another piece of the puzzle dropped into place. Earlier that evening, they had reached the conclusion – well, Lee had reached it – that the object of the oath – the Pride, the Honor, the Glory – was the Cumberland Cup, which the club had received in 1908. So, obviously, the oath could be no older than that. Now, with the help of this yellowed clipping, she also knew the last date that the ritual could have been performed rather than merely recited: December 13 – or probably December 11 or 12, 1941. No cup, no ritual.

And this was a terrifically important thing to learn. Taken with what the charming, delightful Emily LaLonde had told her, it turned everything they knew, or thought they knew, on its head.

'I know who murdered Hamish Wyndham,' she breathed, hardly believing it herself.

But there was one more thing to check, and that too would be found between the Cordovan-leather covers of the massive book. She leafed back to the start of the official members' register, in which every new member from the first grouping of twenty-one on February 8, 1905, to Emily LaLonde on April 10, 2005, had inscribed his or her name. She turned the thick, stiff pages slowly forward to the 1930s, pausing at July 16, 1934, where the twenty-one-year-old Hamish Virgilius Wyndham had signed his name in the ledger – not in the crabbed, spidery hand she would have imagined, but in a beautiful, assured, flowing script, the handwriting of a vibrant young man. Even Hamish had been young once, like every other old person. And there, seven or eight lines above Hamish's entry, with a date of October 20, 1933, was the equally youthful signature of Philip Babbington, whose 'i's were dotted with fussy little circles.

But it wasn't Hamish or Babbington she was interested in. She flipped forward: 1937 . . . 1939 . . . 1940 . . . 1941 . . . and there she stopped. Her finger moved slowly down the page: February . . . March . . . August . . . December . . . At the last new-member entry before December 13, the finger came to rest. September 30, 1941. She looked with satisfaction at the name written there. *Aahh.* She'd found what she was looking for.

'Bingo!' she said softly. 'Give this lady a coconut.'

And went to find Graham.

'Come again? You found *what* in the logbook?'

'I'm trying to tell you,' Peg said crossly. 'You're not

181

listening.' But it wasn't Graham's fault, she knew. She was so excited at what she'd found that she was babbling. She was trying to tell him everything at once, and all she'd gotten from him so far, and from Wally as well, was a blank stare.

'Okay, let me start again—'

'You didn't find Lee?' Graham asked.

'No, I didn't find Lee, she must have gone somewhere else, but I *did* find—'

'Where would she have gone?'

'How would I know that? God, you're exasperating! Look, come on up to the library with me, and I'll show you . . .'

'Okay,' he said, standing. 'But let's have a look for Lee first. Then you can show me what you found.'

Peg sighed. 'Fine, wonderful. All I've done is solved your murder case for you. Nothing important. It can wait.'

Twenty-Five

Lying there in darkness as black as the inside of a tomb, gathering strength and collecting her thoughts, Lee considered calling for help, but decided against it. Whoever had hit her might still be in hearing range, and better not to call his – or her – attention to herself. Possibly, he – she – thought she was dead, and if so, better to leave it that way. She'd find her own way out of this.

The pain from her injured head had sharpened but the billowing waves of nausea had slowed and become less overwhelming, so that after a while – another check of her watch: eight fifty – she tried getting up, pushing herself tentatively to her knees – no pain, nothing broken – then standing erect, taking an uncertain step . . . and dropping hurriedly into a crouch again. She had just learned that when you are in an unfamiliar, pitch-black place, and especially when you're frightened, and particularly when you've been hit on the head, vertigo is a serious problem. You can't tell if the floor beneath you is level or sloping; you don't know if your next step will plunge you into an abyss or down a flight of stairs, you have a hard time telling which way is up, even though your feet are on the ground.

She held her hand up to her face, stared hard at where she thought the fingers ought to be, and wiggled them. Nothing, not a glimmer, even after all this time in the dark. Her eyes weren't going to adapt; not to an absence of light as total as this. Fine. She'd look for another source of light. If this was really a hidden passage in the clubhouse, and other people used it, there would have to be illumination. There would be electricity. This was a modern building, after all – or a twentieth-century building, at any rate – and the light bulb was around long before 1905 (wasn't it?), so there ought to be light switches.

She crawled a few feet on her hands and knees, until she came to a wall that seemed to be made of the rough-cut granite blocks that were the basic fabric of the building, uncovered by wallboard or plaster. She moved slowly along it to her left, running her hands blindly over the surface, looking for an electrical cord that she could follow, or, at about the right height, a switch plate. After four knee shuffles to her left, she hadn't found anything. On the fifth, when her left knee came heart-stoppingly down on nothing, she barely managed to keep herself from tumbling over the edge of the flooring and into empty space.

'Whoo,' she breathed, with her cheek and her hands braced against the cool stone for support until her pulse calmed down. Then she reached tentatively over the edge and found another wooden surface seven or eight inches down. A step? Was she at the top of a flight of stairs? A moment's further exploration told her that she was. There was even a metal banister bolted to the wall. All right, now she was getting someplace. Assuming that she was still somewhere on the upper level of the clubhouse (and, considering the short time she'd been unconscious, that was almost certainly the case), the stairs would take her down to the main floor, where there might well be a door, maybe even to the outside. It seemed a better bet than continuing to wander sightlessly around up here.

Tightly gripping the railing, she inched her way down the steps, counting as she went. At the eighth one she became aware of a strange, snorting sound that she couldn't identify. Whuff-huff. Whuff-huff. *If I were a maiden in distress in a fairy tale*, she thought, *I'd turn around and get the heck back upstairs, because that'd be a dragon down there waiting for me.*

The further down she went, the louder it got, and now she

could make out a soft, rhythmic tinkling along with it. At the sixteenth step she reached the bottom of the flight. A scuffle with the sole of her shoe over the gritty surface under her feet told her that she was now standing on concrete, which probably meant that she was indeed on the ground floor. As she stood there trying to place the sound, she gradually realized that she could make out, if only dimly, a stone wall five or six feet from her. There was light – weak and pale, but light! – coming from somewhere, from the left, around a corner in the passage. Now she remained standing still, waiting for her eyes to adapt, and after a few seconds she began to make out the concrete floor under her, and a small, dusty table up against the wall to one side, with some odds and ends on it: a pair of pliers, a half-used roll of paper towels, a heavy screwdriver, and a few other tools and implements. And now she could at last discern her own hands and feet, which allowed her to move with more confidence.

She walked the few steps to the corner and saw where the light was coming from. There was what appeared to be a wooden door set in the wall, with a space about half an inch wide between door and wall, through which the light shone. Embedded in the door, next to the opening, was a standard key lock. Eagerly, she put her eye up against the opening, but there was little to be seen. The door was seven or eight inches thick, and the stone wall even thicker, which narrowed her view down to next to nothing. Still, she could make out a few features . . . Shelves? A metal counter top? Sliding slowly down the opening, she was finally able to see something with clarity. It was about three feet from her face and it was a can of S&W stewed tomatoes, Italian style, one of a long row of similar cans.

She knew where she was. The clubhouse kitchen. She'd wandered through it yesterday, after the beat-the-pro event, in search of a can of pop, which a kindly kitchen worker had provided. The 'door' at which she now stood was the back wall of the huge walk-in pantry. From the other side it was no more than an unremarkable floor-to-ceiling set of built-in shelves. And the huffing dragon? That was the two giant dishwashers dealing with the dishes and silverware (the tinkling sound) from the luau.

So, at any rate, she knew her location. That was the good news. The bad news was that there was no key in the lock. She tried pushing and pulling on the door, with no result whatever, then called out a few times, but apparently the kitchen was empty. Back to the low table she went, hoping against hope there might be a key among the junk on it. There wasn't, but there was a flashlight. And, to her mild surprise, it worked, although the batteries didn't seem long for this world. All right, then, back upstairs. There had to be a way out up there too (there had been a way in, after all), and maybe she'd have more luck with that. The idea of spending the night here, until the kitchen staff arrived in the morning, was highly unappealing. She might be on a tropical island, but the stone-walled passage she was in was *cold*.

She was halfway up the stairs when she decided to turn around, went back down to the table and poked around among the litter of tools on it. She selected the heavy screwdriver and started up again. Whoever it was that had clobbered her might still be up there.

With Peg tagging along behind, Graham went about the search for Lee as methodically as if he were on a police case. Starting on the upper floor, the two of them went from room to room, opening every single door as they came to it, including the mop closet and the two shower stalls in the ladies' lounge. After a while, his obvious concern got through to her and she quieted down. Where *was* Lee anyway? What was she doing in the clubhouse in the first place?

When they opened the door to the billiards room and stepped in, Peg glanced quickly around the bare room, and then turned to leave.

'Something's funny about the fireplace,' Graham said. 'It wasn't like that before. That opening . . .'

Peg glanced at it, did a double take, and goggled. 'The

telamons!' she blurted, leveling a trembling finger at them.
'The what?'

'Graham, this must have been the library in the old days!
They must have moved the books and the shelving, that's
all! Why didn't we think of that? Why didn't we . . .?'

Graham was shaking his head. 'Peg, I don't know what's
up with you tonight, but I'm not understanding a whole lot
of what you're talking about. I wish you'd—'

'Graham, would you please, *please* just shut up and listen
for a minute? This is important!'

He nodded, but he was obviously impatient to get on with
looking for Lee, so Peg hurried through an explanation:
about the oath, the cup, the moving telamons.

Graham was impressed, but a little perturbed too. 'You
two have sure been working overtime on this. It would have
been nice if you'd been filling me in all along.'

'No, no, we just figured it out this afternoon. We haven't
even seen you since then. But come look at the fireplace.
You see, they've been shifted together, the Telamon of the
North and the Telamon of the South.'

'Which opened up the niche,' Graham said. 'And you
think that's where the cup used to be? Where that tarp – or
whatever it is – is now? And . . .' He reached forward, then
drew his hand back. 'These pieces . . . this is the pool cue,
Peg. Christ, there's blood on it.'

'Yes,' Peg said, not interested in the pool cue. 'But why
is it open now?' Frowning, she answered her own question.
'Lee must have worked it out and gotten it open herself. So
where did she go? Where is she? You'd think she'd have
told Wally. Or you. Or at least . . . Good gosh, now what?'

They both stared at the five-foot length of linen-fold-
paneled wall to the right of the fireplace, which had just
made a clicking noise and now began to swing slowly and
silently outward into the room like something from an old
Charlie Chan movie. Graham got his arm in front of Peg
and moved her behind him. Then, while they watched, the
paneling swung fully open, revealing an opening in which

an apprehensive, menacing Lee Ofsted stood, flashlight in one hand, screwdriver brandished like a dagger in the other.

All three of them spoke at the same time.

'Lee!'

'Lee!'

'Graham! Peg!'

Graham jumped to embrace her. 'Lee, what happened?' His fingers went gently to the side of her face, now swollen and purplish. 'Did someone hit you? Are you all right?'

'Yes, I'm all right, it just hurts a little. Yes, someone hit me. I found the cup—'

'You *found* the cup?' Peg said.

'Yes, it was in that little enclosure. I was standing in front of it and he must have come up behind me, and hit me, and then taken the—'

'Who?' Graham said. 'Did you see who it was?'

'No, I didn't. I don't know who—'

'I know who!' Peg yelled over them. 'Damn it, Graham, that's what I've been trying to tell you for the last half hour! I know who hit her; I know who took the cup; I know who killed Hamish!'

Graham stared at her, his arms still comfortingly around Lee, who had begun to sag as the adrenaline drained away.

'Well, why didn't you say so before?' he asked quietly.

Twenty-Six

'You have the right to remain silent and refuse to answer questions. Anything—'

'No, I don't want to remain silent. I'll answer your questions.'

'Anything you say can and will be used against you in a court of law. You have—'

'Oh, that's all right, it doesn't matter any more.'

'You have the right to speak to an attorney and to have an attorney present during any questioning. If you—'

'It doesn't matter. Well, yes, I suppose I ought to give Tom a call at some point.'

'If you cannot afford a lawyer, one will be provided for you at government expense. Knowing and understanding—'

'The girl, Lee Ofsted, I hope she's all right? It was never in my mind to hurt her, but when I saw her there . . . and the cup . . . it was stupid, I know . . . I should have just . . . I don't even know what I had in mind.'

'Knowing and understanding your rights as I have explained them to you, are you willing to answer my questions without an attorney present?'

'Yes, as I said, I have no objection to answering your questions. Can we get on with it, please?'

Detective Sergeant Milton Fukuda slipped the Miranda card back into his shirt pocket and tipped back his baseball cap. 'Well, then, I guess we'd better head down to the station. No, Keoki, I think we can dispense with the cuffs.'

'Thank you, Sergeant, I appreciate that,' said Evan Bunbury, lowering his wrists.

*　　*　　*

At Graham's insistence, Lee had driven with Peg to the emergency room at the hospital in Kona, where her skull had been palpated, X-rayed, MRId, and eventually pronounced intact. She had been given two Vicodin tablets that had made her head less painful but more muzzy, a trade she was happy to settle for. She had briefly dozed off in the car at the start of the ride back, but now, as they passed the airport, she was awake again and trying to understand what had happened.

'Peg, explain it to me one more time. How did you know it was Evan?'

'I didn't really *know* it was Evan. It just made sense, that's all.'

'Enough sense for Graham to get hold of Sergeant Fukuda, and for them to run off to find him in the middle of the night. The morning, really. It's almost two A.M.'

'I was very gratified that they took it so seriously,' Peg said. 'Anyway, I just explained it to you one more time. Where were you?'

'Sorry, I guess I was asleep.'

'Well, no wonder, with what you've been through,' Peg said kindly. 'All right, I'll explain it as many times as you want. First of all, we've been assuming all along that Hamish was the only person who knew what the old ritual meant, since he was the oldest and most senior member – with the exception of Mr Babbington.'

'Yes, that's so,' Lee said with the elaborate precision of a drunk trying to prove he wasn't drunk. 'But he wasn't?'

'The oldest, yes. The most senior, no. You see, during the glow-ball tournament, that little girl, Emily LaLonde, just happened to mention – about forty-seven times – that she was the women's club champion and that winning the championship automatically gave her a full individual membership in the club, even though she was only thirteen at the time. Well, at first that didn't register as anything important, but then I remembered your telling me—'

'That Evan won the men's club championship at sixteen,

so he must have been made a member then too.'

'Oh, you *are* awake, aren't you? That's right, he would have been granted membership then and there, so even though he's younger than Amory Aldrich and some other people, he would have become a member earlier . . . maybe early enough to have gone through the initiation while the cup was still part of it.'

'Right,' Lee said, not quite stifling a yawn.

'So the next thing I had to do was figure out the date of the last day they could have performed the actual ritual, and I found it in the logbook: December thirteenth, 1941.'

'That was in the logbook? I don't remember seeing it.'

'No, that wasn't in there, but the date of the cup's disappearance was: December thirteenth, 1941. And since you could hardly perform the ritual if you didn't have the cup, that would have been the last possible date that a new member went through the old routine.'

Lee yawned again and leaned her head against the cool glass of the window. 'This sounds a little familiar. Did you tell me this before?'

'Once or twice,' Peg said with a smile. 'So next, I went to the members' register, and the very last new member before that date was – ta-dum – Evan, on September thirtieth. I looked for Amory's date, too, just to see what it was, and it was much later, in July of 1943. So when Amory claimed he'd never been through the ritual and didn't know what it meant, he was telling the truth. But when Evan said he hadn't, he wasn't.'

'But did Evan actually ever *say* he hadn't been through it?'

'Yes! You told me that Sergeant Fukuda asked the board about it, and they all claimed they had no idea what the oath meant because they'd been initiated too late. So he lied about it then – to the *police*.'

'Oh, yes, that's right.'

'And besides, he had a hundred chances to speak up and say he knew what it meant, and he never did.'

Lee was getting sleepy again. And confused. 'Well . . . um . . . so?'

'So if you assume that Hamish was murdered over the cup – and as far as I'm concerned that's a given, especially considering what happened to you tonight – and that only one single person in the world besides Hamish knew the secret of where it was, and this one single person went out of his way to pretend he didn't know anything about it, to *deny* he knew anything about it, and Hamish was murdered minutes before he was going to give the secret away . . . then isn't it obvious who must have killed him?'

In her condition it was too much for Lee. 'But . . . but . . . has the cup been right there in the clubhouse all this time, then? So why did they say it'd been stolen in the first place? And why, after all this time, did Hamish decide to tell? And why *didn't* Evan want him to tell? What did he care? Was it the cup he wanted? Then why didn't he take it when he killed Hamish? Or years ago, for that matter? And why—'

'I can only do as much as I can do, my girl,' Peg sniffed. 'One has to leave something for the police, after all.' She drove in silence for a while. 'I wonder if they were able to find Evan. Do you suppose they've arrested him?'

But Lee, breathing peacefully, was out of reach, having plummeted into sleep like a stone into a well.

'Do you mean he was just sitting there at his house, waiting for you to come?' Peg asked. 'He confessed before Sergeant Fukuda even asked him anything?'

'Exactly,' Graham said in answer to Peg's question. 'He was sitting at his dining-room table, drinking port, with the Cumberland Cup next to him, and a loaded, cocked Smith & Wesson .38 caliber revolver on the table in front of him. He was trying to work up the nerve to kill himself.'

'But why? Why hadn't he tried to get away with the cup?'

'Because he was sure Lee saw him. He said you looked right at him, Lee.'

'No, I didn't,' Lee said.

'No, you probably did. You suffered a concussion, you know.'

'I did?'

'That's what getting knocked out is. And when that happens, nine times out of ten you wind up with retrograde amnesia. You completely forget the last few seconds before the blow that did it. You don't remember being hit, do you?'

She thought. 'No, I guess I don't. As far as I remember, I was standing there with my hand on the cup, and then . . . then I woke up in the dark.' She shivered, and Graham put his hand on her forearm and gently squeezed.

'Have some of that coffee,' Peg instructed. 'You can use some caffeine.'

It was 9:30 A.M. on a sunny, breezy morning. They were at a glass-topped table in the huge, marble-floored, open-air lobby of the Outrigger. They had just gotten caffe lattes and a basket of pastries at the coffee bar, and Graham was filling them in on the night's doings. Unshaven and still in the previous day's clothes, he hadn't gotten back from the Kona police station until two hours ago, but he was upbeat and talkative. Lee, in contrast, was feeling subdued, drained, even apathetic. Peg was Peg, eternal and unvarying.

She had already confidently diagnosed Lee's low-spirit-edness as a physiological counter-reaction to last night's adrenaline overload, but Lee thought that seeing her own bruised, swollen face in the bathroom mirror when she'd awakened was what had done it. The bruising could be helped with makeup, but unless that lump below the corner of her eye went down in the next two days, she was going to get married looking like a squirrel with a nut stuck in its cheek. At least, knock on wood, there was no sign of an impending black eye.

'I don't get it,' Peg was saying to Graham. 'If he thought she saw him, what good did he think it would do him to bean her and leave her in the passage, unless he was playing for time? And if he was playing for time, why wasn't he on the next plane for destinations unknown with his precious cup? Why was he just sitting around his house waiting for you?'

'And if he wanted the cup, and the cup was right there all this time,' Lee asked, somewhat restored by the coffee, 'and if he knew where it was, why didn't he take it years ago? And why did he want it anyway? And what—'

'The cup hasn't been there all this time,' Graham said around a mouthful of croissant. 'Hamish was putting it back when Evan killed him.'

'Putting it *back*?' Peg exclaimed. 'Putting it back from where? And does that mean he had it all these years? Well, did he? And why would Evan kill him to stop him from putting it back? And— Graham, why are you just sitting there? Why aren't you answering any of these highly pertinent questions?'

'I haven't just been sitting here, I've been eating this ham-and-cheese croissant,' he said, getting the last of it down and wiping his fingers with a napkin. 'And waiting for a chance to get a word in edgewise. Look, Evan talked for more than two hours straight – they had to change the tape three times – and he pretty much covered all the bases. So how about if I start from the beginning? Wouldn't that be simpler?'

'Good,' said Peg, and Lee nodded.

Graham took another croissant – chocolate this time – from the basket, bit off a chunk, washed it down with a slug of latte, and began. With verbal footnotes from Wally Crawford, who came by to see how Lee was doing after the previous night, the outlines of the story emerged.

Twenty-Seven

'The relationship between Evan Bunbury and Hamish Wyndham went back to the thirties, when their families owned neighboring sugar plantations and their fathers were members of the Royal Mauna Kea. Hamish, in his early twenties, was handsome, dashing, and athletic, famous in the islands as a regional golf champion and a high-ranking tennis player, and the ten-year-old Evan worshipped him. Hamish returned the adoration by treating the boy with kindness and affection, and as time went on and the age difference between them became less significant, they became friends. Evan, fiercely emulating his idol, competed in youth tennis tournaments without success (he was overweight even then) but did much better at golf, where a little extra flab wasn't so much of a handicap. In September 1941, by virtue of winning the men's championship, he had indeed become what was then the youngest person ever admitted to full membership in the club. As Peg had cleverly ferreted out, this turned out to make him the last person to undergo the full initiation ritual, including the uncovering of the Cumberland Cup.

'In the anxious, uncertain aftermath of Pearl Harbor, with fears of an imminent Japanese invasion running high, the club's board of directors was divided over what to do with the cup, if anything, to protect it from the perils of wartime occupation. Hamish and Evan, being young men of verve and resolve, decided to solve the problem on their own by taking the cup from its hiding place and burying it some distance from the club, and from civilization in general, in a disused watermelon grove at the island's barely populated northern extremity.

'That, by the way,' said Graham, interrupting his own narrative, 'was the source of all that reddish earth that was found in the billiards room. It wasn't from the feet of a gang of ritual killers who'd been tramping around the Kapa'au area; it was from the oilskin sack the cup had been buried in for over sixty years. And Wyndham had it on his jacket because he'd been carrying it in his arms.'

'But why . . .?' Peg began.

'Patience,' said Graham with a warning scowl, and took up the story again.

'Solemnly swearing (according to Evan, they'd taken a blood oath) never to reveal what they'd done or to dig up the cup without the other's agreement, both young men kept mum throughout the uproar over the cup's disappearance, and things eventually quieted down. Not long afterward, the beautiful Kathy Mahnerd entered their lives when her parents joined the club, and the two friends promptly fell in love with her. The pudgy, teenaged, lovesick Evan was no competition for handsome, grown-up Hamish, who married Kathy in a grand ceremony at the club. Devastated, inconsolable, the lovesick Evan ran off to join the Navy, where he served with distinction and remained until he was mustered out at the end of the war.

'When he came back, his friendship with Hamish was renewed, but now there was a biting undercurrent of envy; Evan had by no means gotten over Kathy, who was to remain the love of his life.'

'I didn't know that!' Wally said. 'Didn't he marry someone else?'

'Yes, in 1945, on the rebound, right after he came back. Lasted a year and a half, ended in divorce, and he's been a bachelor ever since, pining away for what he couldn't have.'

'This would be a beautiful story,' Peg said, 'if it didn't have such a lousy ending.'

'Evan claims that in all these years, Hamish never once

suspected he was still in love with her,' Graham said. 'And that he – Evan – never made a pass at her, and I'm inclined to believe him on both counts. Apparently he and Hamish did stay close friends all this time.'

Wally confirmed that this was true, and Graham continued. 'After the war, the club and many of its members were pinched for funds, and a serious search for the cup started so that it could be sold and the money used for maintenance. But both men, young as they were, were staunch traditionalists. Better to leave the cup where it was until better times came around, than to risk its being sold and lost forever.

'Better times did eventually come, but over the years there never seemed to be the right time to bring it back. Moreover, it wasn't the same Royal Mauna Kea any more. The standards had been lowered. There were women in it now, and Hawaiians, and vulgar social climbers like Bernie Gottschalk. Without ever putting it into words, they came to the conclusion that the club didn't deserve the cup. And so, for want of a better idea, it remained where it was, and the two men grew old, their friendship strengthened by the secret they shared.

'Then, in early 2005, everything changed. One week after Hamish and Kathy's sixty-third anniversary, Kathy died. Hamish, like a lot of men who have been married for most of their lives, could stand neither to be alone nor to take care of the things Kathy had always handled so competently. Their one child, Grace, lived and worked far away on the mainland and was, in any case, not the nurturing type. In his loneliness, Hamish married Sally Mehai Templeton – according to Evan the first sympathetic and available female he came across.

'Evan was quietly, improbably outraged. He'd lived his whole life worshipping Kathy from a distance, envying Hamish's good luck but never resenting him for it, or so he claimed. And now Hamish, who had had the wonderful fortune to have had her as his wife all these years, had (in Evan's view) despoiled her memory by coming back from a trip to Honolulu, only a few months after her death, with a brand-new (well, somewhat shop-worn) wife – an ugly, dim-witted, forty-something health-care worker, and a half-breed Hawaiian to boot.

'Seething with anger at his old friend and at life in general, Evan decided that he'd had all of the island he wanted. Sticking by their old vow not to dig up the cup without the other's approval, he told Hamish that he wanted to recover it, sell the diamonds and rubies in New York, share the money with Hamish, and then never have anything to do with him or Hawaii again. He demanded Hamish's agreement.

'What he didn't tell Hamish, though,' Graham said, 'was that he was in dire need of the money. His investments, mostly in Internet-related stocks, had tanked when the tech bubble burst in the nineties, and the guy was wallowing in debt that he couldn't see his way out of. All he had was the equity on his house, and he'd borrowed on that to the max. He was trying to sell it to get his money out.'

'Yes,' Lee said, remembering. 'Lynn Palakahela told me she was working with him on something. I guess that's what it was.'

'Hamish asked for some time to think about it, but he apparently came to the conclusion that, while the club wasn't what it had once been, it was where the Cumberland Cup rightly belonged, whether Evan thought so or not. At the board meeting on the morning of the Centennial Ball, when Lynn brought up the subject of the ritual, he saw his chance to get it back in its niche without having to reveal his part in removing it in the first place. He would dig it up on his own, surreptitiously put it back in the niche, and pretend to find it there during the walk-through – to his own "amazement."'

'Wait, wait, wait,' Lee said. 'How can you know that? How can you, or Evan for that matter, know what was in Hamish's mind?'

'We can't,' said Graham. 'We're guessing at this point,

of course, and we never will know. I'm just taking a few liberties to fill in the gaps. But it all adds up. Evan was immediately suspicious of Hamish's intentions when the older man so suddenly announced that he would walk the club members through the ritual. That afternoon, before the ball, he went to the burial site in Kapa'au and was horrified, but not surprised, to find that the cup had been dug up. Then, at the start of the ball, he went to the fireplace niche in the billiards room: also empty. So he stuck close to Hamish during the affair, and when Hamish left to, as he said, get his bifocals out of the car, he got up after a minute and followed him. Not seeing him in the parking lot, he assumed – correctly, it would appear – that Hamish had gotten the cup from his car, crept around the building to the kitchen under cover of the darkness, and had gone up to the billiards room via the hidden passage.

'Storming upstairs, he found Hamish in the act of putting the cup back. Evan's rage got the better of him, and before he knew it (or so he said) his old friend lay dead at his feet. At that point he panicked – but not enough to forget to break the pool cue into three concealable pieces, to get the cup back into the niche, and to stuff the sack and the pool cue in there with it.'

'And then later,' Peg said, 'after he "un-panicked," he decided to go back and get the cup after all?'

'Yes, during the glow-ball tournament, when he figured nobody would be around.'

'Except me,' Lee muttered, her hand going to her swollen cheek. 'But there's still something that doesn't add up. If he thought I saw him there, why didn't he just turn around and walk out without doing anything? Either that, or kill me? Why leave me alive, take the cup, and then go home and wait for the police?'

'Because he wasn't acting rationally. In the first place, he says you turned and saw him just as the molding he hit you with was coming down on you, so it was too late to hold it back. Then he panicked again—'

'Evan does that a lot, doesn't he?' Peg said wryly. 'He's really not the type that should go around killing people.'

'You're lucky he didn't decide to kill you,' Graham said to Lee. 'He dumped you into the passageway to get you temporarily out of the way and give himself some breathing room, but by the time he got back to his house with the cup, he realized it was hopeless.'

'Because I'd seen his face, or so he thought,' Lee said softly.

'Right. And that's the end of this sorry story. Who wants another latte?'

Everybody wanted another latte, and Graham signaled the coffee-bar attendant for another round.

'So there was a hidden passage,' Peg was unable to keep herself from saying. 'I knew there had to be. Even though *some* people refused to believe it.'

'Hidden passage,' Lee mumbled into her fresh coffee. 'Can someone tell me why a golf clubhouse even *has* a hidden passage?'

'Oh, I can tell you that,' Wally said. 'I went and found the old plans, Lee, and they showed it. It was originally a service and delivery entry from the back of the building to the kitchen and upstairs to the library – what's now the billiards room. Then when they did all that remodeling in 1965 they put in another delivery entrance and closed off the outside door to this one and walled it over. That left the segment between the kitchen and the billiards room. That's your secret passage. I never could find it, but it sure didn't take you long.'

'I've always been lucky,' Lee said with a crooked smile.

Five months and two days later, on a blustery November afternoon, five people, bundled into the kind of heavy coats not often seen in the Hawaiian islands, stood huddled in a surreal landscape of swirling mist and barren, snow-dusted terrain.

From the looks of it, they might have been at the top of

the world, and in a sense they were, for Mauna Kea, near whose summit they stood, is the tallest mountain in the world, measured from its base 18,000 feet below the surface of the Pacific Ocean. Even the part above the sea is far from inconsiderable, looming 14,000 feet over the lush, green land below – land totally invisible, and almost unimaginable, on this particular cold and cloud-swathed day.

They were there, these oddly matched people, for a ceremony: board members Lynn Palakahela, Amory Aldrich, and Bernie Gottschalk of the Royal Mauna Kea Golf and Country Club, along with and Mr and Mrs Graham Ofsted. Two other invitees, Grace Wyndham and Wally Crawford, had declined.

They were on a cinder-cone-studded plateau a few hundred feet short of the summit, on the edge of a little-visited, shallow green pond known as Lake Waiau. In her hand Lynn held the primitively carved basalt figurine thought by some to represent a man with a paddle, by others a man with a rainbow above his head, and by others an abstract sea turtle, but known to almost everyone as the Mana Stone. It had been removed that morning from the Cumberland Cup and replaced by a beautiful Wedgwood cameo of Augustus Cumberland, ordered by a much-chastened Bernie Gottschalk at his own expense. The cup, with its handsome new ornament, now rested in a highly secure glass case bolted to a wall in the Old Bar of the highly secure Royal Mauna Kea clubhouse.

Lynn held the figurine high, faced the lake, thought for a moment, and with a flourish threw the figurine far into it. Then, in a deep and fervent voice Lee had never before heard her use, she recited:

> *'Kuahiwi nani 'oe e Mauna Kea.*
> *Aka aia i Kohala*
> *Home ho'okipa malihini.'*

'What does that mean?' Bernie asked humbly.

'It means, "You are a mountain of beauty, oh Peak of the White Mists. Take back now the sacred object which has

201

been so long in Kohala but is rightfully yours, and bring us peace at last.'''

'Beautiful, just beautiful,' said a greatly affected Amory, putting on the sheepskin-lined hat he had taken off for the ceremony and re-tying the earflaps.

In silence, they turned away from the pond and began the trudge back to the parking lot near the observatory, through biting spatters of snow.

'Lynn,' said Lee, who had noticed an odd expression on Lynn's face as she translated, 'what does that *really* mean?'

'You want a literal translation or a general one?'

'General will do.'

'It means,' a smiling Lynn said, checking to make sure that Amory was out of earshot, '"It's *snowing* up here, for Christ's sake, so how about going home and putting this ridiculous baloney behind us, and getting on with our lives?"'

'Amen to that,' Graham declared, squeezing his wife's gloved hand.